Dear Steve,

Thanks for the memories,

all the best,

Trev

FOOTPRINTS

Trevor Warman

authorHOUSE®

AuthorHouse™ UK Ltd.
500 Avebury Boulevard
Central Milton Keynes, MK9 2BE
www.authorhouse.co.uk
Phone: 08001974150

First published by AuthorHouse   5/17/2010

ISBN: 978-1-4490-9623-6 (sc)

This book is printed on acid-free paper.

For Candice, thank you

PROLOGUE

The sound of pattering feet woke me from a light and troubling sleep. As I rubbed my eyes awake, a bright white light immersed my face and senses. I felt greasy and hot as I fell back on the mattress. I wrenched the cover over my head, only to feel it being yanked away from me, out of my grasp. I surrendered and opened my eyes, to see the face of an angel and a bright white light, streaming from behind her head. Was this heaven? It must be…then my senses kicked in and reality flooded me. It was my daughter, Madison, standing at the bedroom window, in front of a world carpeted with snow.

I started thinking of the day ahead and the errands I had to complete. My head pounded from the night before but, as Madison ran down the stairs and called up to me, my heart filled with joy. I felt a child again, begging my Dad to take me sledging on the hills.

After getting up and plodding downstairs, I wrapped myself in warm clothes for the day. I took my first step in the snow. Crunch…a beautiful, velvet carpet destroyed by my size 11 boot. We skipped across to the park, Madison slipping on the ice, falling and laughing. I could hear her voice so happy and excited as she threw snowballs at passers-by and parked cars.

I turned and looked at the bare trees, iced with snow, moving with the whispering wind. As I pondered this beautiful scene, I felt a crack in the face and tasted moisture in my mouth, as Madison giggled to herself. I chased her, following her footprints in the snow. I ran and ran, until darkness surrounds me. I am fighting against the wind, treading through water until my legs give way with pain and I fall to the floor. I realise that I am not in the park; Madison is not in front of me. My head swirls, my eyes open and I am back in the sterile room as the steel door in front of me clanks open.

I wake up; covered in sweat as I feel for the side of the bed. My breathing is fast and my heart is pounding like a bird trying to escape from the treachery of my body. Like a soul trying, helplessly, to rid itself of guilt.

I sit up and realise where I am. Those soul aches that steal us from sleep return, duller and angrier than ever. The steel clank of the opening door drags me back to actuality. I wait for a figure to appear in the doorway and for the next part of this dark episode.

1

Canterbury

"She arrives in fifteen minutes; I am heading down to the station now. We'll meet you out if you're around later on?" I say, slipping on my trainers and racing for the door.

"No worries! Later on." Brad, my housemate replies.

I rush out of the door, busy and frantic, across the railway lines to the station, where she will be. Three weeks, it's been. Three weeks! No more hour long phone calls, hanging up and calling back because our credit is running out. No more texts and picture messages, navigating the 400 miles our bodies longed to travel. She was coming. .....finally.

London

Jo was a wonderful girl. She was a 21st century woman all right, yet still touched by innocence and sweetness; it was as if her aura was composed of nothing but pureness and goodness. A strong description I know, but Charlie was so used to seeing girls in this area destroyed by drunken men and plagued by premature desires of family and childbirth. Some were sedated by their parents, attempting to rectify their own shortcomings, through the lives of their children. Jo seemed to transcend all of that. Of course, she had enjoyed the flights of fancy her city nightlife had afforded her. She would have some skeletons in her closet and have regrets like everyone else. But as Charlie looked at her in this moment, none of that seemed to matter.

She looked over at him and pondered how to spend the following few hours. She barely knew him but he intrigued her. The decision she made, as often happens, was the wrong one.

The train pulled in, bringing with it a hum of excitement. There were commuters at the end of their arduous journey, revellers reaching their Friday night destination and lovers meeting after time apart. Often though, unlike the movies when couples meet, we don't run and kiss, dropping bags and twisting bodies. We acknowledge each other with a peck on the cheek and turn towards the town. We are older, more controlled, even fearful, though the fires still rage underneath the surface.

"What a cold day! Shall I carry your bag for you?" I say, wanting to say more, wishing I could think of something more intelligent.

"No, no it's fine." She flashes a smile. "Who is at the house?" she asks burning for the answer she wants to hear, a quiver in her voice.

"No-one." I turn to her and smile, our hands link and the uneasiness begins to pass. Our shoulders raise and the pace quickens homeward.

Charlie watched her from across the bar. She knows me, he thought. She has seen me here, with the others.

He got up from his stool and hurried up to the toilets. In front of him stood two cubicles. One door was ripped from its hinges, the other was occupied. He waited, planning in his mind what he would say to Jo later on.

The lock released and out bustled a burly man in his thirties. Charlie smiled as he walked past, before sliding into the cubicle himself. Charlie firmly closed the door behind him. He waited for silence before pulling out his wallet and a twenty pound note. He fumbled for a wrap in the side compartment. He opened it up and laid the contents on the toilet seat, neatly arranging it into two lines. It was this buzz that kept him young, kept him feeling alive, he thought to himself. He heard footsteps up the stairs. It could be anybody he thought, so he would have to be quick. He rolled up the note and put it to the seat. He breathed deeply letting the cocktail fill his lungs. Pupils dilate, blood releases. He flushed the toilet, breathing back, once again. His heart rate increased and his head felt clear as he unlocked the door to see a twitchy young man standing in front of him, waiting for his cubicle. He smiled at the nervous lad and felt like he was part of some secret society, where you communicated with other members via nods, smiles and sideways looks. He felt for the first time in a long while, as if he was beginning to matter as he turned and walked down the stairs thinking of how he was going to get talking to Jo.

I put the key in the door, my hands shaking, cold and nervous. A wave of panic ran through me as I placed her bag on the side.

"Fancy a tea?"

"That would be lovely," she replied, still unable to let her guard down. After all this time and the nerves get worse. I move into the kitchen and flinch at the mess on the side. I can only imagine what she must be thinking. She was always a very clean girl, Bobby. Why had she come? She had travelled half the country for this?

As I sifted through the fetid smell of crockery to find something remotely palatable, I felt her arm at my back, her hand on my side. I turned around and saw her in front of me. Her pupils dilated and the rush of blood. I held her and pulled her to me, but before I realise, she is on her knees, tearing at the buttons on my jeans. I worry because all I can think of is the mess! She doesn't care though as my hardness fills her mouth and we close our eyes together.

Charlie arrived back downstairs and looked across the bar. He saw Jo chatting with friends. The trick was when she paused, where would she look then? He waited until her beautiful mouth stopped. Slowly, hesitantly she lifted her gaze. He quickly caught her eye. She smiled shyly and cautiously. Jo was always good with people. She was confident in situations, always able to make someone feel comfortable.

Luckily for Charlie, the powder was beginning to take effect and he was gearing up to make his move. He knew a few of Jo's group through social circles. After all, this was a small and depressing suburban town. The only major relief was the social outlet of the clubs and bars. The interaction with others and the realisation that you are not the only one feeling desolate and alone was something of a heart-warming experience for the twenty-something's of Sutton, Surrey.

Charlie, in essence, was a small town playboy. People who knew him well tended to like him, some however, hated him. His manner put you at ease, if you were with him. Yet, there were a plethora of girls and spurned boyfriends who had it in for him, largely due to his exploits over the years. He caught the eye of Adam, (one of Jo's entourage) whom he knew from his university days.

Charlie made small talk with him, learning about his city job, his third floor flat and the new Ford Focus he had bought on HP. Charlie shuffled nearer to his prize for the night and watched her as she finished her drink.

"Can I get you another one of those?"

"No, that's fine." She replied sweetly, passing a polite smile his way.

Charlie knew that was that with Jo. A 'come on' is a 'come on' in any language, in any town all over the world and she was not interested.

Charlie sloped away, visibly deflated...

"Actually, sorry, I will have an Amaretto and orange juice…if that's ok?"

"Sure," Charlie smiled, "no worries."

Sex is great, I thought. No doubt about it. But the feeling you get from a good blow job; that's amazing. There's no narcotic in the world to beats that.

I sat on the sofa, flicking through the TV mag.

"Lost, maybe later at 9. Or possibly that Heroes thing everyone is on about at the moment?"

"Hmm, yep, if you like. I just want to spend time with you hon. It has been so long." Bobby replied.

It's strange, you can convince yourself that you are solely in love with one person, that you need them, send soppy messages and verge on tears. But as soon as you come, it all changes and you just want to get the fuck out of there.

"Me too, babe. Me too." I remembered. "Or we could head out? Catch up with the others?"

"What! Brad and Ben stoned in a pub somewhere? We should give it a miss, I think."

I slouched further into the chair as I felt an oppressive hand rubbing the top of my head.

2

Jo's place was impressive. The gear had kicked in nicely and thus the mundane, became fairly exhilarating; none the less though, she had an impressive place. It was a three-bed roomed house, built on a new estate known as Belmont Heights. Her Mazda convertible sat outside. At 22, she was the image of success.

She let Charlie in and showed him into the front room. As she went to fix drinks, Charlie placed himself on the sofa and fumbled for his wrap in his wallet. Again, he made two lines, bigger this time, knowing what was coming. Jo entered with a bottle of vodka and glasses. She saw the paraphernalia on the table and smiled, glazed-eyed at her man.

She kneeled down slowly, taking the £20 note slowly between her thumb and forefinger. Charlie noticed her nails, bright red, perfect attention to detail. She looked *so right*, no wonder she had accomplished so much. And here she was with him! Charlie couldn't really believe it, but if he had learnt anything from his fleeting encounters with women, it was always to try and exude confidence. Women will forgive a multitude of sins for a man who appears in control, who appears powerful. She passed the note to his shaky hand. As he lent down, she moved beside him and kissed his neck gently. He smelt her scent, while he inhaled the white powder in front of him. His head cocked up and his eyes rolled back. A warm glow overcame him as he caressed Jo's hair while she moved on top of him.

The pub was busy with students out for a cheap night and locals watching the football. I could see from the outside the fogged up windows and the neon lights, that always felt as if I was coming home. I guess that is the thing with not having a home. Places of comfort, that are solid, that don't threaten; become your substitute. This was The Tenet, my local and essentially, my safe haven.

Not that the Tenet was a boring, Sunday afternoon pub. It was the mainstay of most of the students in the city and thus one was usually guaranteed a rather interesting night out. Students, on the whole, are guaranteed to do a few things. Firstly, they would get hammered on a night out. Secondly, they would most probably pull. But in our case, we were a little different. Because our university was so near to London and also because it was not one of the 'Red Bricks' or more established institutions in the country, it was guaranteed to cater for a certain type of clientele, like myself. Coming from the streets of East London, where surviving is your main criteria, you could expect a slightly different university experience and one that the other students in this town would not be expecting, one that was littered with violence, drug taking and a certain degree of debauchery.

Charlie made love to Jo for most of the night. Actually, the reality was that she made love to him. From the moment she moved on top of him, in the living room of her beautiful house, she controlled the night. It was a beautiful experience for both of them; their bodies moving together locked in time. They were fuelled by the adrenaline and chemicals in their bloodstream, as if they were the only two lovers in the world and they only had the night.

Charlie woke to the faint smell of burning arousing his senses. He thought that breakfast may be ready or that next door's car maybe needed a look at. But as he slowly opened his eyes, he looked down at the white sheets on the bed as smoke rose from them and a red hole burnt deeper into the duvet.

Charlie jumped up and managed to grab the piece of burning glass that was causing the problem and managed to throw it out of the window. Charlie looked around and saw the room covered in candles and remembered the night he had just had.

Jo arose in the panic and saw what had happened. She burst out laughing at Charlie's reaction and the absurdity of the situation. Charlie looked at her, at first angry and aggrieved, but soon her angel's face melted away his acrimony and he smiled too. He pulled the curtain, to view a crimson morning sky.

"Ah, man…I don't know…I am 21 years old! What the fuck am I doing staying in and watching rubbish on the TV? I know she has just come down, but do me a favour!"

The boys smirked.

"Yeah. I mean she only travelled half the length of the country, gave you a nosh and now you have left her indoors, in our shitty mess. I think that's fair!" retorted Ben.

We all broke into hysterics.

"Bullshit! You have a right to be out enjoying yourself. You invited her out, she just didn't fancy it. Her choice. Anyway, you won't be young forever and your mates will be around longer than Bobby will."

I gazed into the distance and thought about what I had done. It did seem harsh. I felt like a cruel bastard. I had better go back and get her. At least make a call. I felt the coldness of my pint on my fingertips and a brush on the side of my hand. I looked down to see Brad crumbling a brown powder into my drink. I looked at him in disbelief and smiled.

"Ah, come on. The night is yet young!" He pleaded.

I swilled my drink and looked at Ben. I drank deep and smiled over at the girls looking at our table. I'll phone later.

Charlie and Jo headed into town. Charlie was light-headed and chatty. He never really believed in whirlwind romances but he was in the powerful clutches of one. And this was a girl he had seen and wanted for a long time. The coke was still charging around his system too, adding to his buzz.

The two of them walked and chatted, hand in hand, and it was as if their problems just evaporated. It wasn't often life felt like this; savour it, Charlie thought, it won't last forever.

They got into town and held up in the bar that was the opening scene for them the night before. It always felt strange going back to the place you finished up in only about 10 hours ago! It was completely transformed and the elixir of sweet perfume that hung in the air during the night was replaced by the faintly repellent smell of stale beer. He ordered drinks, Jo had a white wine and Charlie ordered a lager; always tricky after a heavy night, but why not? He had reason to celebrate.

As they sat and talked, they seemed to really hit it off. Jo was a fascinating woman. Charlie learned that she was half-French and was fluent in the language. How exotic, he thought! He talked about their families. He hid as much as he could about the dysfunctional mess his had become and she spoke fondly of her university days, keeping the gory details to herself, selling it as if she had glided through the three years like an elegant lady dancing through a ballroom.

Charlie's phone buzzed with a text. He paused until Jo had finished before he checked it. It would be the usual Sunday text, he guessed, one of his mates wanting to know how he had got on last night. Unfortunately, this was not the case.

It was his ex-girlfriend, whom he had very tentatively agreed to meet for a drink that afternoon. It read:

Hi hope you feel better. Are we still ok to meet? I can be there at 1pm and can pick you up on the way. X

Charlie looked up and saw Jo's face, anxious.

"Anything interesting, hun?" She asked coyly. Charlie was in a predicament; should he lie or come clean here and now? He had had relationships in the past predicated on lies and he was determined not to let this happen again. However, he knew how he would feel if the boot was on the other foot.

He decided to come clean knowing that after the initial upset for Jo, it would probably be in his best interests. It was a worry though, he had clean forgotten about that meeting and he knew full well that his ex, Helen, had every hope of them to getting back together. He felt a dark cloud descend upon him and a pain in his gut. To make matters worse the hangover was kicking in and the drugs were wearing off. He looked at Jo, pleading for an answer, as she stared into the distance.

I finished my beer, swilling it at the bottom to ensure the powder dissipated fully into the liquid. The powder was always strong and I was at the mercy of how much my so-called 'pal' had put in there. Anyway, as my old man would say, 'this is not a rehearsal' and that's how I viewed these days, as a platform for experimenting and general narcissistic behaviour.

"They seem to be doing all right over there," I glanced up at John, our landlord. I felt in recent weeks I had spent more time with him than I did at home!

I looked back at our table and saw Brad and Ben re-enacting some story to three girls from our University. Their story almost certainly involving me, as they looked up at me, smiling and talking behind their hands. Pair of cunts, I thought. Here I am buying them drinks and they are ruining my chances tonight.

I got the drinks and went back to assess the damage, but before I could, I was tapped on the shoulder. I flipped around to see Jen, a girl from my course. She was beautiful and blonde with big green eyes.

"I didn't know you were going to be here tonight, what are you up to?" She asked.

"Hi Jen. Nothing much really just a few drinks with Brad and Ben." I pointed over at them. They smiled and waved back to a chorus of *'Hi Jen!'*

How embarrassing, I thought. They don't miss a trick to make me look stupid, these boys. She laughed and waved back at them. "We're going to Lasers later on if you fancy it? Bring Tweedledum and Tweedledee too, if you like. I've got free tickets."

"Nice one, I might just do that!" I said smiling at her trying to gauge her intentions here.

"Cool. Grab me later on babe and we'll sort it out." She said as she turned away.

Here's hoping, I thought.

The situation with his 'ex' was a serious problem. Helen and Charlie had had an intense relationship for what was pushing five years. It ended in rather tumultuous circumstances, largely with Charlie's tongue in another girl's mouth and then Helen's fist in his face.

It was a bizarre story, but following a work night out for Charlie, he decided to go on with a few colleagues to a club. He was happy to get himself home later on, but Helen was pestering him, saying she would come and pick him up and so on. He told her she didn't need to but she insisted. The friction between them at this stage of their relationship was great and she didn't trust him at all. Rightfully, so it turned out.

She decided to go to the club where he was and wait outside until he was ready to come out. According to Charlie, there was no agreement at this stage to be picked up, let alone a timeframe. As Helen became more anxious and time wore on, she decided to take matters into her own hands. She stormed to the door of the club and demanded that she be let in by the bouncer. Now nine times out of ten, a bouncer would say' no' to this request, but in this case for some reason, he let her in.

Helen searched around the club for the elusive Charlie, not being able to find him anywhere, until she spotted him on the dance floor, entwined with his work pal , Jackie. She had always worried about their relationship and inevitably, she was proved correct. Rage swept through her body and she punched him repeatedly in the face, causing a massive furore in the club and even more trouble to follow.

It was easy to jump to a conclusion and call Charlie all the names under the sun but there is plenty more to learn about their fiery relationship in this story and in all honesty nothing was ever cut and dried with the pair of them...

Anyway, Jo left the pub to let Helen speak with Charlie and as time grew nearer to 1pm, Charlie became more and more nervous and afraid of what was going to happen. Essentially, he didn't want to hurt her, but every time she came around, he had no option but to, as she refused to take 'no' for an answer.

Charlie scrabbled for his phone and searched his phonebook for his sanctuary, his saving grace. This was the number that always rang. The phone that was always answered.

"Hello."

"Hi, it's Charlie here. I need to pick up."

"How many?"

"Two…"

"Where are you?"

"Sutton, High street."

"Ok. I'll be there in 45 minutes."

"Cheers."

The line went dead and Charlie breathed a sigh of relief, he looked up and heard Helen's voice, "Hello Charlie."

I felt myself begin to warm up. It was odd; a gooey, hot feeling in your chest and a feeling like a switch in your brain being activated. My legs started to tremble from the increased energy. I could feel my pupil's dilating. Ben was talking to me. Rambling on and on at pace. A pace you only really reach when you're off your head. I was nodding and looking interested and things were fine as Brad tried to roll a cigarette with little luck, due to the sweatiness of his fingers and palms.

"So are you coming then? We are getting a cab now?" It was Jen. I looked up and she saw my eyes and she chuckled. I looked at Ben and he nodded.

"Sure we don't want to go home now, what do you reckon Brad?" But before I could get an answer, the boys were already arm in arm with Jen's mates on their way out. She smiled at me, "Come on then , trouble", and took my hand. I could hear my phone in my pocket. I ignored its death knell and headed for the door.

3

"But we were supposed to be getting married. What about that? What about that! I love you Charlie, you know I do…"

Charlie was fading fast. Helen was brilliant, a pass master, at getting the guilt to rise up in you to the point where it almost consumes you. He wiped the sweat from his brow.

"I know you do…and I do too…it's just, things have changed. We can't be like this anymore. It's not healthy for anyone."

Helen had hold of his hand across the table. She stared deeply into his eyes, her bottom lip quivering and her make up running. She had lost weight to be fair. She had made a real effort. He could fuck her this afternoon…he mulled it over and thought better of it. How many times had that happened before? What would it do to her? They had been in this situation for about 16 months now. She would always go back. He would always submit under the pressure, the guilt and they would always have sex. It would even, always be good, but it could only be so good when you knew the storm that lay ahead. After every time there would be this grinding of minds, one stuck in the past, loyal and forgiving like a beaten dog. And the other; guilt-ridden and hurt, but crying, fighting and screaming for freedom.

"Just say Charlie that this is it! Say it! You bloody can't can you, you prick! Because you want this, you just won't…commit!"

Charlie was caught out, thinking of Jo's breath on his skin last night. The heat of her thighs straddling him in the living room, that brilliant waiting, the glorious anticipation.

He looked across at Helen's desperate face and he felt pity. He was used to this. It was what always brought him back. Last Christmas he planned on finishing with her for good, after another trial separation. However she had turned up with a bundle of gifts; a pink jumper, a

Russell Brand DVD and the pity took over again. He knew he shouldn't. His friends told him that it was damaging her more, but they hadn't been there over the last five years. They didn't see her good points.

At that moment though, he felt a frightening sense of desperation. He wondered exactly what lengths she would go to, to get her way and it seriously frightened him.

"Look Helen we end up in the same place every time. You won't ever get over Jackie. I have apologised so many times. I have tried to move us on, but there is always the sly comment, the tears in the bathroom, there is always that indecision! You don't really want this; you just want…something. anything."

With that he felt he had broken an unwritten code. He wasn't allowed to be so blunt. To put the cat amongst the pigeons like this. He waited anxiously for the response, any response. Helen nodded, got up and walked out. Charlie felt, for the first time in a long while, free.

I was beginning to buzz a lot now. It's an awesome feeling, like being completely out of control. My heart was racing, eyes wired, and jaw pumping furiously on the chewing gum I had got off Jen. In this moment nothing and nobody really mattered at all. I was zoning out, staring out the cab window, watching the rain drops on the window splinter the light outside.

I came back and noticed the group were talking rapidly, yet passionately. We were all in the groove, a mix of drunkenness and drugs swirling in a moment that felt so perfect, but will never be remembered.

I looked down to notice Jen's hand on my leg as we sat tight in the cab. I wondered whether she even realised, she was probably high too. She must have felt my gaze on her as she swung around, out of her conversation, to smile at me and squeeze my leg. Just when I thought that I couldn't feel much better, a wave of pleasure washed over me.

The most difficult thing about doing drugs is getting into the club. There was a class A substance stuffed into the sock of my shoe, plus my eyes were like saucers and all bouncers are keen to mug off someone who is clearly off their nut. Having these girls with us helped though. I had been chatting to Jen pretty much solidly, while Ben and Brad created a light-hearted backdrop to proceedings. They were generally fucking about with Jen's mates, picking them up, flirting outrageously and it was great. It kept things light-hearted as I wanted Jen badly, but I knew she had someone back home in Essex. She also knew about my situation. However, I didn't think she'd be overly-thrilled to know I left the other half indoors. Anyway what she didn't know…

We made it in, despite the boy's loudness and daftness and Jen stayed close by me. I went to the bar and got a round in for the lads while Jen had a vodka and orange. The powder was causing me to sweat, I needed to get into the toilet and sort the gear out. The boys saw me and followed me in wanting a dab or a toot of the powder, no doubt.

"I wonder how your girlfriend is?" Brad smiled, I couldn't really sense his tone. Sometimes he seemed annoyed with my antics. He could talk!

"Which one, Brad?" asked Ben, "The one sitting at home waiting for him, or the one he is going to bang tonight?"

The boys laughed together as I locked the cubicle behind me and reached into my shoe. It was always tight, three men in a cubicle but not the end of the world. And anyway, needs must.

"Fuck off you two. As if anything will happen with Jen. She has that Dagenham rude boy. Nothing will happen."

I had the most unbelievable capacity for self-denial, for doing the worst things, yet only seeing the propensity for good in the actions.

"Anyway, what about you two? Those girls seem all right?"

Ben just giggled, while Brad dabbed furiously at the wrap.

"I definitely wouldn't rule it out," Ben said. He seemed distracted and I could see him reaching into his jeans for something.

"What you doing, having a tom…?" But before I could finish, he pulled out a glass container, which seemed to be filled with a clear liquid.

Brad smiled as he realised what was happening. I was worried about tomorrow and the mess, serious mess we were about to cause.

Charlie finished up his pint and left the pub feeling somewhat invigorated. Yes, there was an element of fear, but also there was a sense that he may get another chance. To change his life, he knew he had to shrug off Helen, but it was so hard. He had little willpower and lacked that cruelness to really get rid of her. But it seemed this time, that maybe, she was working it out.

Charlie waited for his dealer. This is what he called downtime and was a complete waste of time. He kept the same dealers he had had since he was 16 and for some reason, never really managed to 'upgrade'. So he waited indefinitely, which was frustrating, although he always felt the wait was worth it. Luckily, the boys who dealt to him, tended not to fuck about with him so much. He did happen to know the main dealer, Robbie. He had just become too big to be driving around the local area dishing out gear to the local idiots. Plus, he wanted to keep a low profile after a rather nasty brush with a gang of gypsies a couple of years back.

Robbie was just making his way in this world and was like any young guy with too much money. While Charlie and the rest of his pals were finishing school, Robbie, was beginning to learn the tricks of the trade. How to use baby-teething powder (to make the gum's go numb), how to wrap, how to cut, how to give 0.7 or 0.8 of a gram every time, to make a profit. However, he was a lovely bloke, thought Charlie. He probably still is. People automatically think that dealers are degenerates from estates, scraping up rat poison to cut their stuff with. This was never true with Robbie. He came from a 3 bed semi in a nice part of town. I think, in a way, he regretted the way his life had panned out.

Anyway, Robbie, was beginning to do well and make a name for himself to the extent he was providing cocaine for three fairly major towns in the local area. He was generally going out on his own doing business, thinking that the less people that knew, the less risk, and the fewer problems.

Yet he wasn't afraid to spend a bit of money here and there. He bought himself an Audi A4 and was on the point of getting a boat. He was treating his mum too, here and there, but in his naivety, he was also attracting some rather unwanted attention.

He got a call, one night and went on his own to deliver. Three guys ended up bundling in his car and driving him onto their caravan site. They were undesirables who had heard about Robbie's success and felt that they wanted a part of it.

They got him out of the car and threw him on the ground. With a couple of razorblades they proceeded to slice his face across the nose. Robbie thought his time had come. After giving him a kicking, they nicked his gear, his phone and left him bleeding in the middle of the site.

Robbie now has three drivers all getting a fairly hefty wage, about £200 a day to answer his phone and do the deals. So if anyone fucked Charlie around and left him waiting, he would call Robbie who would give them a rollicking, something they really didn't want.

Anyway the guy turned up. Charlie hadn't met this one before and he had, from a distance, a couple of people in the car. As he drew nearer, Charlie realised there was a girl and what appeared to be a baby in the backseat.

"All right?" He said, a bit nervous and pensive.

"Hi. I haven't met you." Charlie retorted, getting an overwhelming sense of his own importance.

"No I am pretty new. You know Robbie then? He reached into his baby's pram and pulled out a pair of socks. He unravelled the socks and pulled out two wraps. The relief of scoring was dulled by the sadness of this scene.

"Yep. We go back years." Charlie reached for the gear and handed over £80. Charlie was struggling to hide his disappointment in this guy. Charlie knew there is always that sense of shame with drugs, but when you bring the innocent into it, it becomes even more shocking; even more abhorrent.

"Cheers bro."

"Cheers." He sped away, the baby jolted in the chair and Charlie felt a real emptiness as he headed for the pub toilet.

"You see, it's a difficult situation really. We have been together for ages, but here I *find* we are growing apart"

"I know. I feel guilty constantly. But, everyone else seems to be doing it and then ,although I know it's not all right, you feel, it is?"

This was going great. I was rushing massively, but Jen didn't seem to notice. She was pouring her heart out about her scumbag boyfriend and how she felt. I guess a problem shared is a problem halved.

"My old man, always says to me this is not a rehearsal, you know. You may not get another chance to do what you want to do. I guess he's right."

I realised that what I was saying was pretty risky but I thought Jen was on board. *Fuck it*, even if she isn't. You don't know unless you try.

She breathed deeply. "I guess we both need to sort out our situations, huh?" She looked up at me and smiled.

"I think you're right."

With that, she took my hand and led me through the crowds of people by the bar, across the dance floor and into the girls' toilets. She checked for a cubicle, found one and pushed me inside. It's an amazing feeling, when you know you really should *not* be doing something. Anyone could have seen us. *Anyone.* For all I knew her other half and mine were here together to get us both. Maybe they were. I had to get a grip as I knew it was only the paranoia kicking in.

I pulled Jen closer. She was passionate and warm. I could taste the sweat on her lip as we frantically pulled at each other's clothes. She sat me down and pulled out my cock. I was amazed to find I was hard, a testament to how much I wanted her. She positioned herself over me and sat down gently, softly. I felt her warmth surround me and to be honest, guilt was the furthest thing from my mind.

Jo and Charlie had spent a pretty chilled day in the local pub. They watched West Ham play Man United. It was Alan Curbishley's first game in charge of West Ham and they had a shock win, so Charlie's spirits were high. They had met up with Tom, a friend of Charlie's, who was a temperamental character and was seemingly getting more and more irate. Charlie and Jo just held hands and smiled on through his diatribes.

"It is not immigration *per se* Charles that is the problem. It's the scum we let in. It's the countries they come from and their lives over there. Do you think these fucking eastern Europeans have any concern for our ideals and values, for respecting one another? They are out there killing themselves and that way of life finds its way over here. That's the problem."

Tom continued but it was difficult for Charlie to listen. It was odd when you found a new lover, all the stuff you used to find interesting goes out the window. Tom was still talking, he may well be right, but what's the importance in society's problems when you are falling for someone? When you think someone sees something special in you?

"I don't know, Tom. It all sounds a bit fascist to me. What do you want to do? Barricade the gates? Paint 'no entry' signs on the white cliffs of Dover? It's a slippery slope mate…"

Jo was getting bored with this. She knew where it was heading. She had seen it all before; the ranting, the raving, the wogs, the pakis. Her time as a barmaid left her numb from the rubbish 'the locals' spouted about so-called politics. Their ignorance frightened her a bit.

"Exactly! England's full. It's not like we are the size of America anyway. And they screen people so not every dirty, pilfering cunt gets in there. You know what I mean, Charlie?"

Charlie smiled at Tom. Normally he would start in on him, but he had company and quite frankly bigger fish to fry. He touched Jo's hand, running his fingers down hers from the fingernails to the inside of the wrist. She smiled at him and leant forward to kiss him. She tasted sweet, it was probably her lip-gloss or her drink, but at this moment he knew it was just her; she was perfect.

4

I woke up in my bed, fully clothed. I opened my eyes and turned around to notice a familiar lump beside me.

"Hey babes how are you?" I whispered knowing the response really.

"Just fine, I spent all night in, on my own! You crawl in past three. Not a text, not even a fucking call to see if I am ok. Yep I'm great. You prick."

Fairly standard response I thought. Got to take that on the chin really. I was most definitely still feeling the effects of the night. I felt like I was floating on air, hovering two inches above the bed.

"Well it works both ways. You could have rung me and we could have sorted it out." I retorted, not really wanting to fight, but not ready to back down either. Anyway, what *did* happen last night?

"I fucking did, but your phone was off for half the night!"

Then it dawned on me, Jen! Please tell me she hasn't been through my phone. Where the bloody hell is it? I tried to appear calm as I scrabbled down in my pockets, to find it, thankfully in my jeans pocket.

"Sorry, hun. There is never any reception in the pub. I…ah…I'll leave you to it." I said as I rolled out of bed and down the stairs. I heard Bobby harrumph and turn over as I left the bedroom. I frantically grabbed my phone. It was off. A real saving grace, otherwise I could have found myself in big trouble. Ben's bedroom door was wide open but he was nowhere to be found. It was 10.30am, chances are he was not back yet.

I meandered downstairs, still off my head. The sun was shining and I didn't really care about arguing. As my phone fired up, I put the kettle on and sat in the kitchen. I felt good. There was always that initial buzz that still remained after a heavy night, where the hangover was in the post, but had not yet arrived and the drugs were still coursing through the veins. I felt a little bad about cheating with Jen. In the cold light of day, my father's advice seemed a little idealistic.

The phone buzzed. I had three messages. The first read *come home baby, I want to sort this out. I love you x x x.* The guilt was beginning to creep in. I was having such a good time last night *I didn't even check my phone. I was truly a prick.

The second was from Ben, *mate, at this quality party with B-rad give me a bell come down.* That would solve the mystery of Ben's whereabouts. I decided to reply, *Are you still copping off with Brad or are you two love birds coming home soon? Xxx.*

He would love that, any gay references sent Brad a bit mad. Ben was more in touch with his feminine side, but Brad couldn't really get to grips with that type of banter.

The third message was Jen and it was not what I expected. It read, *let's pretend that none of this actually happened I feel so bad not good if I could go back I would do. If anyone finds out about this we will both be in trouble sorry I know this is weird for both spk sn x.* It came through at 4.03am so that would explain the garbling, but she was really defensive. What did I do? What happened after the club?

"Everything all right honey?" A voice asked from behind me. This was a white flag and I was taught from an early age these don't come around very often in relationships, so take them when you can.

I got up and put my arms around Bobby. She started crying and whispered into my sleeve "I love you. *I love you".*

I dutifully held her tighter as my phone buzzed. It was Ben. *Yeh, we have pub golf later on today. Need a shower, see you in a bit, stud!*

Bobby loosened her grip and wandered back upstairs. Here we go again, I thought.

For the next few weeks, Charlie tried hard to clean his act up. Truth be told, the situation with Helen had taken its toll on him. He used coke essentially to sustain himself and the nights out he felt he needed, to give his life some purpose. If he was out with friends or chatting to girls, Charlie felt alive. At home alone in his flat, he felt like he was just well…wasting away.

Charlie had lived on his own for six months before he met Jo. He had previously lived with a friend in the local area which was an eye-opening experience. His pal, Donny, lived in a rundown and squalid flat. He was a 40-something city worker. To be fair he was out most nights with 'work' but Donny was single and as such, spent no time improving/maintaining where he lived. Charlie saw it as a vicious cycle. Don wanted nothing more than a lovely woman to settle down into middle age with. In this day and age, it probably wasn't out of the question for him to even have a kid or two. But he spent no time or money on himself, his clothes, his flat, because he didn't allow himself to. It was his defence mechanism. If anyone asked him why any aspect of his life was the way it was, he would just respond with how *busy he was with work* and how he *didn't have time*. Charlie was not so sure.

Anyway, Charlie could only take so much of the living arrangement with Donny. He came to the conclusion that after a while guests started to smell like dirty socks and he felt their relationship straining. Not to mention the fact that Charlie managed to have relative success with the ladies. This irritated Donny, as Charlie always felt the need to clarify the state of the flat because, in a way, he was a little surprised at the way Donny lived, even though he was a good pal.

After a couple of months, Charlie looked into buying his own property and managed to move into a small but well decked out one bedroom flat. Granted it was not the Ritz. It was not even half the size of the place he used to share with Helen, but it was his and he was beginning to enjoy staying there. He kept it tidy. Obviously not 'woman tidy', but he did well for a 20-something, making sure he hoovered when it was dirty and aired it when it smelt.

Charlie felt the need after the break up with Helen to be out socialising as much as possible. Truth be told, in the months after the break up, she was around quite a bit too. She did have some capacity to be normal, but she always had the propensity to fire up and get angry or breakdown when things got on top of her. But he felt the best he had done for a long while. He still found it lonely when he stayed in. He always searched his mobile for numbers he could ring to try and get out, but in the end he was comfortable and, given the turbulent past, comfortable would do.

He spent an increasing amount of time with Jo, either at the flat or at her home in Belmont Heights. Although it was a nice house, it was maintained fairly poorly. She and her friend never really had any food and, with a lot of new-build houses, the walls were thin; every step on the staircase, every bump in the night–reverberated around the house. One night they spent giggling to themselves, as they both heard her housemate use her vibrator in the early hours of a morning.

This morning they had planned a picnic on Primrose Hill. Charlie found himself doing things he never normally enjoyed; cruising down the aisles in Tesco with Jo in hand, picking out meats, soft drinks and toiletries. Charlie was always a little fearful of this level of domesticity. He was worried that the free spirit, the libertine within him, would slowly die if he became a true consumer, all settled down and worrying about the price of petrol. The truth was he felt freer now than he ever did before. He was amazed at the power of love. He watched Jo pick something off the aisle ahead of him. Her blonde hair perfectly shaped, the cut of her jeans, the tan on her shoulders. He breathed deeply and thought maybe people *can* change for the better.

They rode the train up to town and talked freely about the future and what they wanted from life. Underneath the veneer, they were both educated people with good jobs. Charlie was a school teacher and despite his problematic social habits, he was good at what he did. He subscribed to the philosophy that by having problems in school himself, he was able to understand the troublesome students more. He could relate. It was all about understanding. In fact everything is about understanding, he mused to himself.

Charlie had been expelled from school. He never took authority well and found it very difficult to accept people in power doing a bad job. This had caused him problems throughout his life. Whenever he was told off, he would end up digging himself a hole by arguing and being disrespectful. This experience had allowed him to see the error of his ways and he felt he could pass this onto the obstinate kids he taught who did the same. It usually worked.

He didn't really get on with most teachers for the simple reason that the majority of them were rather plain. He didn't have a great deal of sympathy when the staff moaned about little Jimmy squirting water, or swearing at a TA. He sympathised with the students on the whole and felt that generally, the kids were all right.

Jo was a recruitment consultant and consequently earned quite good money for her age. She again was a natural at her job. She had the gift of the gab and warm tones which prospective clients instantly liked. But she longed to do something with a bit more substance. The thought of making money for a faceless company didn't sit well with her and she wanted a change.

Charlie listened intently as she spoke of a teaching job she did a few years back, in Thailand. It appeared she was thrust into a backwater Thai school where she was given no training and essentially told to teach. She said by the end of it she had really made a difference to those kids' lives and cried when she had to leave.

At the moment though, they were making more money than they knew what to do with. Charlie couldn't see Jo sticking in recruitment however. Although she fit the role superficially, she wouldn't be able to do it forever. Nor did he want her too, as he could see it made her largely unhappy. At the moment though hand in hand, walking through North London, she couldn't be much happier.

For most of the day I felt awful about how I'd treated Bobby. I was well aware I was in the wrong, but on the whole it was just an oversight. I had meant to ring Bobby and sort the problem out but I was enjoying myself too much. Bobby wasn't really the type to wish me any fun, unless it was with her. This is why she would never have come to meet me last night and that's why we had been at loggerheads all morning.

The other issue was that of Jen. The answers are fairly easy really. I am a bastard, a prick, a selfish, male chauvinist with no concept of emotions, feelings or commitment. But as I drew these conclusions that were shouted from the rooftops by every jilted woman through the history of time, it didn't quite wash.

The first problem I have with this is that Bobby and I were not right for each other. This fact had plagued me for a while. The second was that I was at university and in the same way we are told that 'cheating is bad,' I found myself surrounded by people at university telling you to *live your life, to be free, to take risks.* You only have your university years once; you have the rest of your life to *settle down.*

The third is (and it's not a popular theory) that it is a genetic flaw of men. I am often told of the need to procreate, spread the seed etc. and I don't fully subscribe to this theory. However, if you throw into the mix, drink and drugs, it is very difficult to stop yourself. Needless to say, all this rationalising didn't stop me feeling guilty. I could vaguely rationalise my actions but it wasn't really enough.

So, Bobby and I had decided to go for a drive to the coast. I wanted to treat her a bit, make sure she understood that I did love her very much and I wanted her to feel happy. I toyed briefly with the idea of owning up to her about Jen, but given Jen's text, it didn't seem necessary. So I took Bobby for a meal and tried to make last night up to her.

"Listen, I am sorry about last night. I totally accept responsibility for not checking my phone and…"

"Charlie, listen. You are entitled to see your friends and have a good time, but not at our expense. You know how much I love you." Her blue eyes bore into me. "I know when you are angry or hurt you put up your barriers and want to run a mile, but it's ok, I understand. We just need to talk more."

I winced at the buzzwords. Talk, understand, *barriers*. Also this was perceptive and it cut a little too deep.

"Anyway, I want to go out tonight, this pub golf sounds fun. Let's move forward darling."

"Ok!" I smiled at her. I hope she couldn't see through me. I am pretty sure she didn't.

"At work, there is something I want to discuss with you."

I knew very little about her job in Leeds. I knew she worked for Goldsmiths' jewellers, but from what I was aware she had a pretty smooth ride.

"Ok…"

"There is a ring ,honey, and it has just come in. It's an old engagement ring but it's pretty perfect and the lady wants a quick sale. She was left by her husband a month before their wedding and she wants us to get a price for it as quickly as we can."

"Right…"

"Well, with my staff discount, I can pick it up for about £250. It is probably worth somewhere in the region of £2000! It's exactly what I want!"

"Sounds pretty good!" I tried to sound enthusiastic.

"Well, what I am saying is I think I should buy it and…when you're ready to ask me, you can…give it to me? And pay for it obviously, y' know. I just think it's such a good deal!"

What could I do? I looked at Bobby beaming at me across the table. I really couldn't do this now, I felt bad after what I had done and essentially, this decision was too big to make here and now, at this stage of my life.

I thought I should tell her about the night before but, in a way, if I was to let her buy this ring it could make things better, maybe start a fresh page for us. It would help me…atone?

"Baby…" she said softly, "what are you thinking?"

"I am a bit surprised," I said tentatively, "…but, I think it may be a good idea…"

"That's so good Charlie, I knew you would be pleased! Because you know what baby? I have already bought it for us! I pick it up when I go back tomorrow!"

5

Primrose Hill was beautiful in the summer sunshine. The two lovers lay back on the grass, drinking champagne serenely, in a blissful setting. Charlie looked over at the view of Camden Town. He was a Londoner by birth, having been born in Mothers and Babies hospital in Woolwich, South London. Well, at least this is where he was *told* he was born. On the day when his father decided to take him there, a day that would stand out in Charlie's life to help give him a sense of identity, they encountered one major problem his father had missed. The hospital had been knocked down some years prior to their visit to be replaced by blocks of flats. This didn't surprise Charlie, he was just glad it wasn't a Tesco.

Despite this, he was a Londoner through and through. Although he was an educated young man and prided himself on his fairly broad general knowledge, he spoke in a rough and fairly abrasive, south London twang. He had lived in suburbia and took every opportunity to get into town whenever he could. He believed strongly in the London music scene and followed his local football club. Now, he cherished moments of sheer tranquillity on Primrose Hill, sipping champagne. He felt safe and without a care in the world.

"You know Charlie, we should do this more often," He felt the sun-kissed warmth of her skin as she leaned towards him.

"I could spend, every day like this…with you…" he trailed off, realising he had briefly let his guard down, something people rarely do nowadays, being too afraid of the rejection that may follow.

"Me too. I am not sure we spend enough time with each other. I think I have had at least…two nights on my own, since I met you! Not good enough Charlie!" She beamed a wide grin over at him. One of the things Charlie fell for when he met Jo was that smile. It could light up a room, turn a situation. Well after all, it had changed him as a person. Thanks to Jo, her vivaciousness, her confidence, her love; Charlie was even beginning to like himself.

"Well there is a way we could solve that…you know..?"

"Hmmm…" Jo replied innocently.

"Well, you could move in?" Charlie again had put himself out there, open to rejection. He felt a real jolt of fear and wondered whether he should lighten the mood by adding in, 'you practically live there anyway,' to the sentence. He didn't. Sincerity seemed to be working for him and he didn't want to mess this up.

"Charlie, I'd love to! I don't know what I'd do without you. I love you y'know?" It was the first time she had said this, although he had felt her warmth and knew it was there. He could have jumped up and down, with happiness, but he held his composure.

"I love you too."

They fell back onto the grass in a powerful embrace, passion flowing through their system, fuelled by heat and love.

To say I was pissed off by Bobby's actions would be a huge understatement. What on earth was she doing? I had heard some bizarre marriage stories in my time, but this was something else. I subscribe fairly heavily to the idea that a man should have the right to choose a ring and give it to his loved one as and when he felt the time was right. This was ruined now. I felt an awkward pressure; a strange waiting and a cocky glint in her eye which wound me up.

We were drinking in the Wetherspoon's pub in town. It was fairly amenable by Wetherspoons standards. You could get served quickly and it was cheap. However, it still had the customary smell of sick around the bar, not to mention the sticky tables and filthy glasses.

Ben had managed to get a fairly good crowd out. The thing with Canterbury was that it was a very small city. It only took us around twenty minutes to walk from one side to the other. On the whole, the Kent University students, stayed up on the hill, where they have plenty to do. We had the run of the town most nights, except when the squaddies from the barracks came in. Then we usually made ourselves scarce.

Most of the Christ Church guys knew each other. If you played in a team and hung around the Union, you would become fairly well known and we were lucky in that we had met quite a few good people and were able to socialise in the same group most of the time.

Tonight, we had decided to give the drugs a miss, seeing as we were having a fairly heavy night on the sauce. That did not prevent Brad, Ben and well, myself, having a few spliffs earlier in the day, just to get us started. I never really thought of weed as serious drug taking partly because I wasn't overly keen on it and also because it was so common in student circles. Most of the time in halls and around campus, you could smoke weed and no-one would really bat an eyelid. This worked well for Brad as he was possibly the heaviest marijuana smoker I had met. There was probably a one hour gap from the time he woke up, showered and had breakfast where he was not smoking weed. The rest of the time he was high. My attitude to it was that this was fine. He was a big boy and it meant that I could have a toke as and when I wanted and I actually quite enjoyed the smell. Not that I had an option with him!

Bobby had come out with us that night. She was to travel back to Leeds the next day, and, on the whole, we had enjoyed a pleasant day. The coast was fairly blustery, but attired appropriately, it was refreshing rather than cold. The sea air was enjoyable and just being there made me feel more comfortable with myself. Seeing something so vast and uncontrollable, made me feel slightly better about the direction in which my life was heading.

Anyway, we were on relatively good terms by this stage. I had waited for her to get ready and had a few vodka and Redbulls while she did so. She looked impressive, her hair spiky and short, and wearing a cute black and white dress. She was always someone I would describe as striking rather than pretty. She had big blue eyes and amazing tits. She was a keen runner, and so had a nice figure, although she did have a tendency to put weight on quickly at times. At the moment she was in between a size ten and twelve, which I liked. I wasn't into skinny girls as it suggested someone who didn't eat, drink or enjoy their life too much. Bobby, when she was in the right mood, on the right night, could be good fun and I really hoped this would be the case tonight.

Bobby was making an effort with some of the girls who were out. She was being chatty and sociable and this helped me relax. I was in a corner talking to the boys about Bobby's revelation.

"So what do you think? Fucked up I reckon. And yesterday of all days after the night with Jen!"

I had it on good authority that Jen would not be out that evening. Although a twang of desire played in me when I thought of her, this was certainly a good thing.

"I think you are in a lot of trouble with this one, mate. Its lose/lose. She is now expecting you to ask her to marry you. If you break up with her, you are going to be accused, if you like, of jilting her. It's a real problem," Brad mused.

"But won't people think she is just mad for going out and doing what she's done?" Ben retorted.

"Well, some will, I guess, but others will think what she did is sensible. Essentially, you are in a long term relationship. A relationship either ends or you go on to get married in most cases. Some women will probably even say it's sweet, or touching that she has bagged a bargain for you, if you like." Ben sniggered.

"You are joking, right? People surely can't be 'ok' with this? It's intrusive, it's presumptuous! It is true that we have been in a long term relationship. But I am hardly marriage material!" I replied, getting increasingly desperate.

"Well, she doesn't know that, does she? Maybe she needs to." Brad replied in a strangely ominous tone.

Charlie and Jo were brought back to reality with a horrible thud. As the vast spaces of the hill, were swapped for hot and sticky commuter trains, the familiar buzz of an incoming text on Charlie's phone, conspired to ruin their day.

Hi Charlie, I hope your well. I have been thinking about things and I realise how much I miss you. We need to talk. We can't just let things fizzle out the way they did. I am sorry for storming out. We can sort this out. Love H x x x

Charlie's heart sank. Despite his new found happiness and desire with Jo, he struggled to really put a definite end to this. He saw a serious fragility to Helen's nature. There was desperation in her words and actions and he didn't want to hurt her too much more. With most people, you can hurt them, cut them down and they will bounce back eventually. With Helen he was not so sure.

"Who is it babe?" Jo knew full well who it was. They had had the conversation about Helen and her burgeoning omnipresence. She could see Charlie's shoulder's sink as he read between Helen's lines. Charlie thought it best not to lie.

He handed her the phone, realising he didn't want to jeopardise his relationship with Jo. Honesty, in most cases, was the best policy he thought. She read it silently and breathed in deeply.

Jo couldn't contain her anger any longer and blurted out, "Can't you just tell this girl that it is over? Is it over, Charlie? Am I just being taken for a ride!?"

"Of course you are not!" Charlie was surprised she could think this. "I want you! You know that, but it's difficult with Helen. I spent a lot of time with her. I nearly bloody married her! Not that I wanted to, well you know the situation, she is…"

With that, Jo broke into tears, holding her face. Charlie went to hug her, but she shrugged him off violently. Charlie was helpless. Like a child wanting one thing, but being told he couldn't have it. He pressed reply on his mobile.

I think this is over Helen. Although we can meet up to talk if you think we should.

No kisses. Cold, but necessary. As he pressed send, he was able to feel Helen's oppressive hand holding him down and preventing him moving forward, as it always had *. He turned to Jo, who stared out the window. A disappointing end to a beautiful day.

The pub golf was going fairly well and it worked on a very basic principle. Essentially, you had 18 pubs (holes) and on each hole you had to do a certain drink (alcoholic) in a number of shots (swigs). Whoever had the lowest score at the end, won. You also had holes with water (where you were allowed to use the toilet) and holes with sand (where you were allowed to be sick).

Today we were only playing nine holes as eighteen can take its toll, especially with girls in the group because with all the equality in the world, most women struggle to handle a large volume of alcohol.

We were four holes down and the guys had the arduous task of a pint of Stella Artois in five shots. I was hoping I could knock this back in four. The girls had to knock back a spirit/mixer of their choice in four.

The mood was good-although some of the girls were beginning to get rather inebriated. This could go one of two ways, usually it went badly. However, Brad and Ben were making good headway with a couple of netball girls we knew from the Union. I left them to it because I knew what reaction I would get from Bobby if I went over to them.

Bobby was definitely feeling the effects of the alcohol. Her face was reddening, her bright eyes widening. Despite this, I could tell she was beginning to resent being there as she had a four-hour train ride the next day. She looked at me across the pub with a certain desire; at least I thought it was. It was hard to tell as she often looked at me with certain intensity and it was difficult to understand what it really was.

I finished my pint in four which I was pleased with, but in all honesty, I wasn't really feeling massively keen to continue drinking. I was tired and still felt slightly nauseated by last night's events. The drugs in particular had left me with a fair case of the blues and that was even before Bobby's revelatory purchase. I wondered to myself why life had to be so complicated. I knew that I had feelings for Bobby. I knew that it probably equated to love. But, I also knew if the situation arose again with Jen or with any other girl that I desired, I wouldn't be able to help myself. I was fully aware of how guilty I would feel. I was playing a dangerous game. Women have been known to cut men's balls off, for doing what I do - so why not stop?

Bobby had moved around to my side of the table and pulled me in to whisper in my ear. She wanted to go home and to be fair I thought we probably should. This was not really a couple's 'thing.' All my friends were beginning to pair off, or at least trying to and the house was empty at present.

I made my apologies and left. I walked through the warm Canterbury air towards home. The sky was cloudless and there was a red tinge to the sky as the sun began to set. Bobby took my hand and asked, "So, what do you think of the engagement ring, hun?"

"I think it sounds like a good idea." I lied again.

"I don't want you to feel like you are under any pressure, y'know, just when you are ready."

It's a bit late for that I thought.

"No worries babe." I smiled at her. She smiled back and squeezed my hand tighter. Perhaps this could work, she can be such a sweet girl at times.

That night, Bobby and I had some of the best sex I could remember us having. She was drunk enough to be full of desire, yet not too drunk to become amusing. She tasted good everywhere on her body, before she pushed me onto the bed, held me down and slid herself on top of me. She touched herself and then placed her fingers in my mouth. It was amazing how things changed when she wanted something. I came in a powerful rush inside her. She smiled at me and, at that moment, I felt united with her, as though nothing would separate us. It even crossed my mind to ask her to marry me then! How simple pleasures appeal to the minds of men.

6

Over the next week or so, Jo spent most of her spare time moving her stuff across to Charlie's flat. She could not believe how quickly things had developed with Charlie. Jo was by no means a promiscuous girl; however she had knowledge of men, had lived with them and dated them in equal part. But this made whirlwind romances seem sluggish!

Jo's outlook on life was unbelievably refreshing, in that she did not judge others for past misdemeanours and thus gave Charlie full reign to change his ways. She knew about his past, she wasn't really worried about recreational drugs, as long as they remained recreational. She really wanted her parents to meet him. She knew that they would like him, as above all else, *she* felt happy and secure when in his arms.

Despite Jo's outwardly chirpy demeanour, she did have one issue that weighed on her mind and that was Helen. Although she didn't feel threatened by Helen, she was worried about the way Charlie dealt with her. He seemed to give her so much leeway into his life, to pull strings and make matters worse. The thought of Charlie and Helen sitting over a table, discussing their colourful past, brought a wrenching feeling to her stomach and tears to her eyes. Yet she did not want to seem weak. She did not want Charlie to know how much he meant to her; not at this early stage at least.

Jo had met Charlie in a whirlwind and it had been less than two months before she had moved in. She could see how people could be shocked at her behaviour but she knew it felt right. Charlie wasn't a walk in the park, but there was a substance to him and a passion they shared that she had never felt before. She trusted Charlie which was a good thing, because she knew that on a nightly basis Helen had been texting him, asking to meet; wanting him. She had fought back tears as she lay next to her love, knowing he was being made to think of someone else as he lay beside her. She was angry at him for letting her get away with this, but she also knew it was part of his softness, the way he let her carry on. She wasn't going to rant and rave at him for humouring her, for that is what Helen would have done to him and what he eventually got tired of. So she waited it out.

Bobby and I slept soundly until around 2am, when I was stirred by loud talking next door. The rooms in our house were decided 'out of a hat' and unfortunately I had secured the box room, which was next door to Brad's. I heard the deep bass of men's voices but couldn't make out what they were saying. To their credit, they were only talking normally, which given how much they must have imbibed, was quite considerate.

I could smell weed through the door. I could hear Brad strumming on his Epiphone Les Paul and quiet music was playing. I looked at Bobby sound asleep and sneaked out to Brad's room.

I opened the door and there was Brad, smiling up at me. Ben was slouched on the bed and Brad's pal, Harry, who hung around us occasionally, was there too.

"Hey man, what's up? Did I wake you up? Brad sniggered.

"No mate, don't worry. How did it go?" I asked.

"I don't know, why don't you ask Ben?" Harry and Brad burst out laughing.

Ben moved slightly, but looked uncomfortable.

"Uh, Ben..?"

Ben sighed before blurting out, "That bitch, Carly, slapped me, right in front of everyone in the fucking club!"

The boys were in hysterics; I think the weed was helping. Brad passed the joint to me, I declined. Ben took it and took a few drags.

"No shit! What happened?" I said.

"She saw me with that netball girl, you know, Kate. I was with her on the pub crawl and at the last pub, I got her number. Well one of Carly's mates told her. The rest is now Canterbury fucking history."

"Or breaking news! You wait until tomorrow, everyone will be talking about it, man. You're fucked. Don't think you're getting laid ever again in this town!" Brad said as Ben grabbed the pillow and hid his head underneath it. We all laughed at him, knowing it would be fine and forgotten by tomorrow. Things always seemed terrible when you were drunk and tired.

At that moment, we heard the familiar sound of Brad's creaky door again. Bobby stood in the doorway, in my dressing gown. She looked at me incredulously.

"What are you doing?" She asked.

"Well…I'm chatting with the guys, finding out what happened. Are you ok?"

"Could you do it any fucking louder, other people in this house are trying to sleep!" The mood dropped as she held her gaze solely on me.

"Well it is a university house. You are not the only person here, Bobby…" I tried to state with a calming tone.

"Yeah but its nearly 2.30! Do you guys have no consideration? I have to get a train back tomorrow, I have work in the evening…"

"So sleep on the train!" Harry said gaily, to no-one's amusement, especially Bobby.

At this point she could take no more. "You are all fucking losers and wasters. No wonder none of you have any girlfriends, you're a fucking shambles!" She slammed the door and stormed back to my bedroom.

Brad looked up at me with a grin on his face. Ben stared into the distance, wide-eyed and clearly a bit hurt. Harry swung on his chair, I thought just thankful that she had gone.

"I better go and…" I sighed, gesturing to the cyclone that had just swept through the room destroying the good humour as it went.

"Yeah, enjoy mate." Brad said, smirking at me. I left the room and felt all the weight of disappointment, embarrassment and anger return like an old acquaintance, just as quickly as it had left. What the fuck was I doing with my life? This can't surely be right; this can't be what it's going to be like forever, can it?

I pushed open the door to find Bobby sitting up on the bed, crying. As I walked past her she tried to grab me around the waist and pull me towards her. I threw her hand away in anger and grabbed my cigarettes.

"I'm sorry," she whimpered. I stormed out and downstairs without a word.

Charlie grabbed the last of Jo's stuff from the car. He had been a different person recently. His friends had said it was due to Jo and it probably was. Whatever it was, he felt more in control of his life. He felt he could achieve his goals and do the things he needed to do.

He rushed up the three flights of stairs with the bags and dropped them in the bedroom. Jo was knee deep in trinkets, towels and sheets.

"I am going to lock the car, hun, I'll be right up!" He said.

Jo flashed a smile at Charlie as he turned for the stairs. It was a strange time for him as he felt he was doing the wrong thing by Helen, but he was excited and happy. He didn't have much guidance and knowledge about relationships as his parents had broken up when he was 13, leaving him fairly despondent about happy endings. He saw firsthand what a break up does to each member of the family. On top of this, his sister had left for university at the crux of his family issues, leaving him to shoulder most of the burden. This had left Charlie angry and resentful. He had never allowed himself to trust someone to that extent since. He always trusted his sister and thought that his family would show him unconditional love and trust when he needed it. She didn't. She left him with the problems and hadn't spoken to him, or even supported him since.

Helen had represented a form of security which helped him fill the void left by his uncaring and selfish sister. She was the first family he had been taken into that was normal, nuclear and accepting. Obviously her parents hated him now after the break up and all the bits involved with it. Yet he still felt a loyalty towards her for letting him in and for making him realise there was a normality to be had, a happy ending if you like.

His phone rang in his pocket. He always knew it was his as he had a very distinctive ringtone. Charlie was not usually one to be drawn into that sort of stuff, yet he had become extremely fond of the band, Babyshambles. He felt that the life of Peter Doherty largely mirrored his own. He too had an odd upbringing. He was estranged from members of his family and had used friendships/bonds to fill that void. He also had used hard drugs to numb the pain left by the apathy of those closest to him.

The ring tone was 'Loyalty song' a song he had become obsessed with, ironically, at the time he had met Jo. Charlie didn't like things like this; he felt it was fate trying to tell him something, that maybe he should go back. He didn't believe in coincidence. He tried to shake himself out of this way of thinking but something always pulled him back.

It was Helen on the line. He answered straight away.

"Hi Charlie. How are you?"

"Hi. Fine. What can I do for you?"

"You seem busy Charlie, moving more stuff in?" Oh god, Charlie thought, she was here. She had probably seen Jo, he prayed she hadn't.

"Yeah, just got some stuff from Mum's. Where are you then?"

"I am parked up, three roads down. Do you want to have this chat?"

Charlie looked around and saw her silver Corsa. He hung the phone up, looked up at his flat's window and headed over to Helen's car quickly.

I woke up on the sofa to the sound of sizzling and the smell of bacon in the air. I looked around at the state of the front room. There was a full ashtray, a couple of empty bottles of vodka and a few beer cans. The room smelled about as bad as I did. I remembered the bottle of wine I opened when I came downstairs. It lay empty on the carpet.

Time is a great healer and although I felt a dull longing for change, I was no longer angry with Bobby. It was not the end of the world; she was known for her short fuse. There was something wrong with us though, as a pair I thought. But I believed passionately in loyalty. I believed that we were just young and in time we could learn to make things work.

Bobby was leaving soon and I felt a pang of desire to resolve the problem before she left. I scurried upstairs to see her and as I pushed the door too, she sat on the edge of the bed, pristine and pretty, ready to go.

"Hi, she looked sheepish and bit her bottom lip."

"Hi, you look good. Listen…I wanted to say…" but before I could finish, she had grabbed me and kissed me long and hard on the lips. It felt a bit wrong, as there I was unclean and shabby from the night before and she looked and smelt quite beautiful. For some odd reason, she liked the smell of alcohol on the breath and cigarette smoke. I never understood it, but it worked for her.

We made love passionately again. As I came hard into her, she said something which I really didn't understand and most certainly didn't take as seriously as I should have.

"I love you more than you can ever know."

Like a true Neanderthal, these words post-orgasm, passed me by, as my mind flitted through all the things I needed to do that day. I would come to regret not listening and not understanding Bobby's passion.

Charlie got into the car and asked Helen to drive away somewhere quiet. He was largely excited by what he was doing, but also felt pangs of guilt and fear because he did not want to affect his relationship with Jo. He was confused to say the least.

"What are you doing here Helen?"

"You said you thought we should talk."

"I said we *can* talk if you really wanted to. Do you think this is a good idea? *Really?*"

"We spent some of the most important times of my life together. I don't want to just lose contact with you all together. I mean, we had a future, before last summer. We were getting *married.*"

"Yes, but things change and things happen for a reason. The relationship was not right, you said so yourself. Why else would the situation with Jackie ever have happened?"

Silence. Charlie knew that whenever this came up it affected Helen massively. He wasn't even sure that it upset her for the right reasons; he was convinced it was because she lost face in front of work colleagues and friends alike.

He remembered a time last year when he had sat down for a meeting in the staffroom with his English department (of course, Jackie was present). He saw Helen run out of the room with one of her colleagues following her. Charlie found out later that Helen had been banging her head, quite literally against the wall and screaming in the next room and had to be forcibly sat and calmed down.

"It was a mistake Helen and I cannot have been the first man to make one. Plus, I have paid for it. The last year and a half has been a string of guilty accusations and recriminations. Do you really think we can go back with all this bad blood?"

"I don't know! I just want to…you know, see how things go?" As she said this, Helen filled with twisted thoughts of the past, moved forward and tried to kiss him. Charlie was confused. He knew there was no going back, but felt strangely compelled to stay in the car, to revisit old ground, to see if the spark was still there. As they moved together entwined, Helen's passion heightened, her breathing grew heavier and she pushed herself further onto him. It was at this moment Charlie's epiphany occurred. It reminded him of the past, her constant need to be in control, yet to be completely out of it. He could feel an overpowering force, a dark cloud he had known before descended over him and his excitement dissipated. He opened his eyes and pushed Helen back into her seat. She looked over at him in disbelief and tried to claw at his clothes as he left the car and briskly hurried home. Helen sat in disbelief. He could hear her cries as he marched up the road.

I walked Bobby to the station and put her on the train. We both got relatively emotional as she left. I didn't like goodbyes at the best of times and for all our rows and bad behaviour, there were some strong feelings between us.

These feelings soon passed as I made my way through the alleys and back to the house. I was still aware that I had to face the rest of the house after last night's incident. I felt sheepish and embarrassed and didn't want to face the boys yet.

As I turned the corner onto our road though, I saw Brad, Ben, Harry and a few guys from the house across the road coming towards me. It was 2pm and Ben was pretty dressed up. I guessed he would be out for the duration of the day and night.

"Hey man what's up?" Brad said. He was stoned. You could usually tell by the redness of his cheeks and the tone of his voice. He also developed a perma-grin across his face. At least you knew where you stood with him.

"Just dropped Bobby at the station. Where you guys heading?"

"Down to town, for a few beers. Give us a ring if you fancy coming down. It could turn into a bit of a session."

"Nice one. Sorry about that shit yesterday. You know what she can be like." I said.

"Don't worry mate. We left you a present in your room. Hopefully it will make you feel better. Ben grinned at me."

"Cheers! I'll be down in a bit."

I liked male company for one main reason and that was that you knew where you stood with pretty much any guy in the world. Yes, arguments happen, problems occur, but generally after a beer, or a kip, issues will be forgiven, forgotten and resolved. I knew it was the last we would talk about the Bobby issue for the time being, unless I brought it up.

I got back to the house and rushed up to my room. Ben had left me a joint, or at least what seemed like one. I smelt it and noticed it had very little scent and it dawned on me. It was a coke joint. I burst out laughing; this was exactly what the doctor ordered. I undressed and grabbed a towel to dive in the shower. It was probably wise to get ready before lighting up. It had probably been about ten minutes since Bobby had left and I felt on top of the world again.

Before Charlie got back to the flat, he stopped off at the BP garage and picked up some flowers for Jo. He knew she didn't like garage flowers, what girl did, but he needed a reason for why he was out so long and the flowers would do the trick. He felt a churning in his guts for he didn't like what he had done. Yes, he was not a stranger to cheating on girlfriends, but it was different with Jo. He had no desire to be with any other female. He replayed the past hour over and over in his head and despite the amount of times he told himself *she* kissed *him*, he still felt bad. He did respond. He was curious. Hopefully, one good thing to come from this would be that Helen would finally get the message and back off.

He came indoors to see Jo sifting through the last of the boxes. She had fixed herself a glass of wine, not a bad idea Charlie thought, given the afternoon he'd had.

"Hello stranger…" she said in a curt tone.

Charlie pulled the flowers from behind his back. "A little present for you for all the stuff you have had to do today," he waited for her reaction. She jumped over the bed and ran to give Charlie a hug. She must have been missing me, he thought. He was so glad to feel her warm embrace, to touch her hair. He never wanted to leave this place he'd found.

"I am exhausted!" She said. "But I am nearly done. What do you fancy doing?"

"I don't know, maybe watch a film, finish the wine?"

"Sounds good to me, give me half an hour Charlie and this will be finished. Ok?"

Charlie smiled. "Ok. I'll put the flowers in water," he said. As soon as the front door was shut and he was at home with Jo, he felt a warm sense of security. It was a new feeling, one that had felt strange and unsafe to him previously. This time he didn't feel like running, he felt that he had arrived at where he needed to be. A year ago, strung out on drugs and booze, he thought he would never be here; but finally he had made a home, a life, a future without Helen. He remembered vividly an argument where she exclaimed there was no-one in the world who would put up with Charlie and his antics. His father had told him that that was rubbish but he always had that nagging doubt in the back of the mind that maybe she was right.

Charlie sat down on the sofa, put on the TV and waited for Jo to come and sit by his side. He drifted off into a blissful daydream, where in the end of it all his friends, his Mum and Dad all found what they wanted, as did he.

Jo came through when she was done and they settled to watch a film Charlie had on DVD, *V for Vendetta*. It was a great film, one of Charlie's favourites, but he knew it was all background for the real action that would be taking place on the sofa. He was lucky, they were still in the 'honeymoon' stage of their relationship and they couldn't keep their hands off each other most of the time. Jo had a relatively high sex drive and Charlie was becoming more and more aware of her sexuality. She was happy to please a man, yet she also enjoyed pleasure; a rare thing in the modern woman. She was also experimental and open to new things which Charlie found a massive turn on.

The wine was going down well. Jo had opened a second bottle for the two lovers. Jo lay in Charlie's arms as he gently stroked her inner thighs and in-between her legs. What he was doing shouldn't really be described as overtly sexual, more sensual. Jo writhed a little in pleasure. She smiled and kissed Charlie's neck as he caressed her.

As they moved together on the sofa the two were thrust from their dreamlike state by the sound of someone shuffling up the stairs of their flat block. There were only two flats at the top and it was relatively late. The girl next door did keep some unconventional hours, so Charlie put it down to that. Yet, at the top of the stairs, he didn't hear the sound of a key in the lock or the familiar creak of next door. Instead he heard what seemed to be a scratching sound. The scratching turned to light knocking and Charlie could tell there was someone there. He pushed Jo from him and sat bolt upright, not knowing whether to grab something or to open the door. A fear rushed through him.

He motioned to Jo to stay quiet and he paused the DVD.

What Charlie heard next will stay with him for the rest of his life. The scratching continued and he heard a woman's voice, a harrowing whimper through the door. The moaning sounded desperate and pained and Charlie's initial reaction was to rush and help whoever was pining outside. Jo held him back. As the wails took form, he could make out the words '*Charlie*' and '*why*' then it suddenly dawned on both of them. Jo held her head in her hands and shook angrily. She got up and rushed into the bedroom. Charlie didn't know what to do. Helen didn't know about Jo and a meeting now would probably not be the best idea. But he really wanted to show some solidarity to Jo. What should he do? By this time the crying had grown louder. It would have unsettled most of the residents in his flat block. It was heart-wrenching, a desperation in the tone he wished he had never heard. He had to do something. He went to the bedroom to see Jo and found her under the duvet. He kissed her head, picked up his trainers and headed for the front door.

As the front door opened, Helen's frame fell into the doorway of Charlie's flat. She was pale, white and her body was limp. She continued to whimper, but she didn't react to Charlie's presence.

"What are you...wha?" Charlie searched for the right words, the best thing to do. He put his arm underneath Helen and scooped her onto her feet.

"Could you...can you try and calm down Helen, we can sort it out. We need to get away from here though." Charlie walked her down the stairs and out of the front door to the flats. He walked her to the nearest bus stop, just wanting somewhere for her to sit, to take the pressure off.

Helen was somewhere else at this stage. Charlie didn't know a great deal about mental illness, but he knew that there was something seriously wrong. For all their problems, he did know the girl very well. She was scared of drugs and he couldn't smell any drink on her breath. But her eyes were gone, unfocused.

"What's up Helen? What's the problem?" He knew he had to be as normal as possible with her, to try and snap her out of her trance.

"It's *you* Charlie…where have *you* gone? I'm alone Charlie…and I love you so much…I can't…I can't do it without you…"

"Of course you can! You're stronger than this Helen!"

At this she burst into tears again and nearly fell off her seat.

"You don't understand what you have done to me!" She spat the words out with venom. "You have taken my independence Charlie. I can't function without you…without us…"

Charlie was losing patience. What was he going to do?

"Have you got your car? Helen, your car?"

"Yeah it's still at the pub."

"Ok, we can go down to it. Then you must go home and have some sleep-you'll feel better in the morning."

"Come with me, Charlie. I want you there with me. Please tonight."

"I can't do it, Helen, it will do both of us no good. There's no point."

"Please, Charlie! I don't, I don't know what I'll do without you, I can't trust myself."

The bitch, he thought. She knew full well Charlie would be worried about her. He had never seen her like this and he knew that she was unstable anyway. What would she do? Charlie shuddered at the thought of what she might be capable of. He checked his watch and it was gone midnight. He couldn't palm her off on her parents or her best friend at this time. *Fuck*, thought Charlie, what a great first night with Jo! He was so dejected; he would not have been surprised if Jo had left by the morning. There was only so much more she could take of this.

Charlie was livid, but he was caught between two fears. The last thing he wanted was to lose Jo, but what if Helen did do something to herself, how could they live happily after that? Not to mention the fact he would probably have to explain to Jo tomorrow. Maybe.

"Ok, let's go. Just tonight though. I mean it Helen, until you can sort things out and get home to your parents or stay at Laura's or something."

"Ok baby, thank you, thank you!" she whispered.

Coke joints were quite different to sniffing gear I thought, wild eyed and stomping into town. It is slightly less harsh and gives you the impression of not being as wired or as edgy as gumming or snorting. It was a nice mellow buzz, but not like weed. You really did get a buzz from the powder.

It was a splendid day as the sun shone down on the old city of Canterbury. It was an historic town and when the mood took, you could not help but be inspired by its fortress walls and the old pubs. You felt truly English on days like today and it was a good feeling. You could imagine old soldiers, going off to war and coming back to feast and drink heartily. They may even get a leg over if they were lucky. It dawned on me that it was not so different to us nowadays. We all go off during the day to fight our own personal battles. Jobs, degrees, looking after the kids, yet we still met in the evening to celebrate friendships and to make the best of the good things in life. The ingredients may have changed, but the objectives were still the same. Through natural or chemical means we aimed to alter our ordinary perceptions of the world and if we were lucky we might find a bit of company for the night. Life was essentially very simple. It was only when we over complicated matters with promotions, mortgages, loans did life essentially become depressing. At university, without a care in the world, how bad could life be? I knew I would pass my degree and the only concern was finding a few quid to rub together to find my next drink.

It's like Peter Doherty. The media, the fans, the hangers-on have overcomplicated the situation to a crazy degree. From what we could ascertain from what we knew of him, he was a man of simple pleasures. He even sings 'I just like getting leathered' in one of the songs. So where is the problem in letting him live his life and getting leathered? It certainly didn't affect my life! The press will always argue that 'he sets a bad example', but if he had no press coverage, then he would be setting no example to anyone. Just leave the guy to write the tunes and be himself and there wouldn't be a problem, surely? God I was wasted, I thought to myself as I trotted to the west side of town, desperate for a nice, cold beer.

7

As they made their way through the dark night, Charlie felt a real yearning. He was a young man, but he was beginning to understand the icy depths and caverns of this world. He had designed his life in his younger years, to limit his pain and be as happy as possible. He wanted to carve out success and decide his own fate. He was beginning to realise this was impossible. He wondered how the tramp, glugging cider, smacked off his face, got like that and he used to feel pity for him. Now he empathised with him because the more you try and control your life, the more it slips away.

Helen glided the car through the country roads of her private school. It was a rich institution set in a valley in the Surrey Downs. At night, though, it felt positively eerie, trees hanging down and not a light or soul to be seen for miles around.

Helen parked and the two made their way up to her flat. Technically, Charlie was not allowed to be there as it was an 'all girls' boarding school and his presence would obviously set a bad example. However, it was late and Helen was past the point of caring.

She sneaked Charlie into her room. It was large and pristine. It smelt girly and homely, the way single girls kept things. There were teddies on the bed and candles on every available space. He thought he could smell incense in the air. She certainly did not live like that when they were together.

It was an unbelievable place to visit as you felt like you were really in the back of beyond. Charlie's father always used to say to him that he loved visiting New Zealand as it was a most beautiful and serene setting. However, you constantly felt out of touch with the rest of the world. It was not dissimilar here as there was not a sound for miles around. There was nothing but darkness out of every window, the phones didn't work, the doors slammed shut and you were completely alone for better or for worse.

This place was the complete antithesis of where Charlie lived with Jo. He was in a real town setting, kebab shop below, a little village down the road and a council estate the other way. This was country living, something he was not used to, but something that interested him, maybe in years to come.

As Charlie's thoughts meandered from here to there, he noticed Helen getting changed by the bed behind him. She had a matching red bra and thong on. He tried not to look at her as she milled about. What was she doing? What was her game? Like any man would, he felt aroused. Her breasts were beautifully rounded and her pale white skin offered the complete contrast to Jo's bronzed beauty.

Helen moved towards Charlie and she stood in front of him with her thong at his eye level. She stroked his head sensuously and out of exhaustion, emotion or whatever it was, Charlie leaned forward and rested his head on her stomach. Before he knew it, he was kissing her and touching between her legs. He could feel her warmth and wetness through her knickers and it spurred him on. He knew it was wrong, but he felt so far away from anywhere, it didn't seem to matter. It was as if they were stuck here in this stasis and tomorrow would never come. Not to mention the fact that in the cold light of day, she had completely engineered this. It was amazing how quickly she seemed to recover from her near breakdown.

They made love that night. Charlie felt turned on by Helen's vulnerability and even her cunning had a certain attraction. She knew what she wanted and she got it. At this moment, Charlie was tired of fighting to do the right thing. He succumbed and let his primal instincts take over.

The pub was lively as it was a Saturday afternoon and the weather was gorgeous. There was a rather large group of us out and even at this early stage, quite a few of the group were going to the toilets on a fairly regular basis. I thought it might be prudent to buy some coke as I had been given a few freebies by the lads recently. Ben could sort it out for forty quid which was the going rate, so I made sure he had a few toots before we went any further.

We had decided to head down to the West side of the city for a change and we were in a nice, olde worlde pub called The Cherry Tree. It was small inside, with an excellent atmosphere, but as the afternoon wore on, we ended up spilling onto the street outside.

What was amusing was that Kate and Carly were both out today. Obviously they were not together but, we all did hang around in one group. Ben was thus keeping a low profile, which was hard for him and against his better nature. However, the more blow he had the louder he became and it felt like it was only a matter of time before things came to a head. He was a good-natured guy, someone I had become good friends with, but like me, he could be volatile if he felt pushed into a corner.

Jen was here with her group as well. She looked pretty good, but I was keen to let sleeping dogs lie for the time being, or at least wait to see what moves she would make.

The night wore on and we made our way to a few of the more decent pubs on the west side of town. Saturday was a quiet night for students on the whole; it was in fact a bit of a surprise to see so many people about. Usually, some students went home for the weekend or just stayed in and saved it for the designated weeknights.

"This is getting a bit dry mate, what shall we do?" Ben seemed anxious, I think he was a bit paranoid from the gear, I wasn't sure it was his drug of choice.

I, on the other hand, felt on top of the world. As drugs go, cocaine was definitely my favourite. You felt out of it, but confident and in control. Paranoia was an issue, but I had been using powder for a while now and guess had learned to live with it.

"I think we should have a party at ours. I am not ready to turn it in just yet," I knew Ben wouldn't like this and in a way I had stitched him up because I don't think he fancied any situation at present where he was in close proximity to these two girls.

"I think that's a great idea!" Ella said, a friend of ours who lived a few roads away.

"Only because you can stumble home when you're ready!" Ben retorted.

"Of course and you have a good stash!" Before we knew it, the news of the party was breaking throughout the group and Ben looked at me despairingly.

"Look, mate, they may not even come and if one does, then you are all right surely?" I pointed out to him.

"Hmmm…we'll see." He put his arm around me. "It can't be that bad can it?"

"No if they cause any trouble, we'll just kick them out, all right?"

"Yeah, although I quite fancy seeing Kate again tonight, she looks good. What about Jen? Is she coming back?"

I really hoped so.

"No, I don't think that's wise. Someone is bound to say something."

"Fortune favours the brave, my friend. How are you doing with that gear pal?"

I pulled out my wrap and passed it to him, I had been fairly liberal with it. That joint had me buzzing all afternoon and with the occasional toot, I managed to keep myself in a happy place.

"Nice one!" Ben scuttled off to the toilet, while I surveyed the scene. It was exciting, watching the different groups come together to socialise. I admired all the different faces, the beautiful girls, the boys trying to get in with them or get away from them. I waited for Jen to move away from the bar, before I got another drink. I didn't fancy seeing her at this stage of the day, but who knew what the night would bring?

Brad, Ben, Harry and I headed back to the house before the others arrived. Though we lived in a shit hole, we had some pride and wanted to at least have a quick tidy, if not a clean up! We had a fair few drinks floating around, four bottles of spirits, and nigh on a case of beers. Brad had a quarter of weed and between us there was probably over a gram of gear and with the help of a few donations from our guests, it could turn into an interesting night.

I put my phone on silent and popped it in my bedside drawer for safekeeping. I had three messages. The first was a 901 from Mum which could keep until tomorrow. The second was Bobby, *Hi sweets. I am tucked up in bed. I miss your arms around me. Ring or text when you are going to bed xxx.*

The third was from Jen, *Hi. I will come over to your party if it's cool?* I instantly replied telling her I looked forward to seeing her soon. I also thought, it might be a good idea to drop Bobby a quick call. I probably had a little while until the rest of the revellers arrived and it kept me in the good books.

We spoke to each other for a good fifteen minutes before I heard the front door go and the noise level increase. I told her I was going to bed and made sure I put the phone down before I was found out.

I got out my powder and made a fairly meaty line on the bedside table. I wondered what other horrors were there on the table, in the dark. I never really cared though. As I breathed in heavily, I felt a burning in my nose and the rush of adrenaline through my body. I was overheating and could feel my heart beating louder and faster every second.

I took a big swig from my vodka and coke and then another, hoping the alcohol would steady my nerves and calm the situation. It did, thankfully. I turned on the light, checked my hair, took some mouthwash and sprayed on my favourite after shave, Lacoste Red. As I opened my bedroom door, there were people everywhere and as I looked across the hall into Ben's room I saw him playing a game in his room with Jen and two other girls.

Jen was wearing a pleated miniskirt and a tight top. She looked fantastic despite it being well into the night. Her eyes flitted around the room and she swung her hair back over her shoulder. She noticed me across the way, smiled and looked down, sheepishly.

Ben saw me and motioned me over to the room.

Charlie awoke to the sound of rustling trees. The light of dawn filtered down onto the bed through a crack in the blind. He could hear nothing, just emptiness and vastness across the hills and valleys of Marden Park. He looked across at Helen sleeping placidly, oblivious to the complications she had caused, the seriousness of what she had instigated.

He suddenly felt alone and frightened. He had no way of contacting Jo. What sort of night must she have had, alone in the flat in unfamiliar surroundings, powerless to stop events freefalling around her?

Propelling himself out of bed, he quickly rushed to put his clothes on. As he did so, Helen stirred. He couldn't face her. What she had done, what she represented. He felt sick, at that moment in time, in the tranquillity of the surroundings. He could smash her face to a bloody pulp. He would probably get away with it and she would deserve it for her ignorance and her manipulation.

"Are you going Charlie? Do you want breakfast?" she nervously asked.

Rage swept up through Charlie's torso. He had never hit women. He had come close but he always managed to stop himself. He wanted to knock her through the wall, it may quell his anger, eradicate what they had done. He refrained.

"Helen ,listen to me. I never want to see you again. I mean that. I don't love you and it is over."

With that, Charlie walked out of the room, as Helen protested, and shuffled out of bed following him. He didn't know what she was saying, he didn't even care. But he managed to shut the door behind him without coming into contact with her.

Despite his anger and rage he knew he was essentially a coward at heart. He still couldn't bring himself to tell her about Jo. For Charlie that felt like going too far. He wished he understood what went on in his brain.

He flew down the stairs and into the empty valley and surveyed his surroundings. The peaks and trees that provided such comfort last night felt intimidating and frightening this morning. Charlie had no means of transport and the only road out of the valley that he knew was a few miles long and brought him out a fair way from any form of civilisation.

Charlie could hear Helen shouting and wailing at him from the window. She was crying and pierced the air with her voice. Charlie sensing himself falling back into old habits, thought of Jo her hair, her beauty, her eyes and began to run. He ran up the hill and into the nearby woods. He had no idea where it would bring him, but he always had a good sense of direction and thus headed towards his home. Many miles stood between him and his goal, plus the terrain was going to be rough, but he knew he had to go, now. He turned back to see Helen leaning out of the window, a tangle of hair, a mess of emotions. It only served to spur him on.

Ben was playing a variation of 'spin the bottle' with two girls, a guy from his course and Jen. They were playing other drinking games too and bottles of beer were being demolished at an alarming rate. We had a bottle of vodka and some diet coke for the girls, although their pace had diminished somewhat.

Jen was definitely a little coy this time around. She was not as forthcoming and in a way seemed to be attempting to avoid eye contact and conversation with me. I didn't think I had done anything wrong the other night, but she certainly seemed to be leading me to believe I had! Anyway, I was so fucked that it didn't really matter. I was coked up and brimming with confidence, so we could just see how it would go.

I fancied another line so I made my excuses and went to the toilet, but as I turned to lock the door, a hand forced the door back.

"Hey, can I have a chat?" Jen asked, with her eyes glued to the ground.

"Of course, are you all right?"

"Yeah, I am just sorry about the other night; I think we got a bit carried away…"

"Yep. You could say that!" I was being a bit of a prick but what the hell I thought, what could possibly go wrong?

"It's not that I didn't want to, it's just, you know, my boyfriend. I felt awful afterwards and still don't feel right. You know? If he ever found out…"

"It's ok, we can keep a secret…"

I looked into her eyes, searching for something. She was really pretty and I could understand her man living away from her and being protective. Who wouldn't be? But this was no time to be worrying about things like that.

"I'm not going to lie, I felt bad too, but I have just…always wanted you."

She looked away again, down at the floor. She was shaking her foot with nervousness.

"I know, me too…"

Before I knew it, we were locked in an embrace again, this time with more fervour and passion than before. Danger was all about us. I was rampant and tore down her panties to feel between her legs. She was moist and pushed herself harder onto me. I put a finger inside her which slid in easily. I could feel her exuding heat as she ripped at my shirt buttons. I slowed her down and suggested my bedroom next door. Jen agreed and we made ourselves presentable for the prying eyes outside, filled with smiles and private giggles. Little did we know that behind the façade of the beautiful people all having a good time, there was jealousy and treachery lurking, waiting to strike.

In the university house we lived in, we were pretty foolish when it came to security. We left the front door open or unlocked most of the time. We had the playstation and TV about 15 feet from the front door. It had never really been a problem. We were up all hours. We were six guys living in a house, it never seemed to really matter.

Or at least it didn't matter until that night, well morning actually, when a presence came crashing through that front door like a tornado and into our house. It swept upstairs and searched the various bedrooms. There were drunken bodies strewn on the floor and on beds, but not the bodies that were being looked for.

I heard my door fly open. The force it was pushed with broke the lock and Jen awoke with a start. The last thing I heard was her screaming and running at the vitriolic male standing in the doorway. He pushed her aside as I tried to raise myself from slumber and into action. It was futile. Before I could remove the duvet, I felt a crack over the back of my head and then upwards onto my jaw. I could see movement around the top floor of my house, people running downstairs, people running towards my door. It felt as if the world had gone into slow-motion as my mouth filled with blood and I slipped out of consciousness.

8

It took Charlie a few hours to get home. He walked through the wilderness and woody land, but after a while found some civilisation, a dual carriageway leading out to the M25 or into Purley. He walked towards the town and found a cab office which eventually got him home. He was greatly worried about losing Jo, although he tried to remain stoical about the whole thing. On the whole, any time spent with Helen made him feel anxious and displeased about 'happy ever after's.

Charlie traversed the steep stairs up to his flat and felt a real sense of foreboding as he put the key in the lock. He opened the door and saw Jo, lying in bed. She stared up at him, from under the duvet as he entered slowly. She threw back the duvet, rushed up and grabbed him tightly.

As Charlie kissed her forehead and stroked her hair, he whispered to Jo that this was the last of Helen.

Jo nodded, disbelievingly and burst into tears.

I woke up in hospital later that morning. It turns out that I was out for a good few hours. My Mum was by my bedside and she looked pleased to see me awake.

"Hi," I tried, but when I attempted to speak it was too painful. Mum winced at my attempt at conversation. I must have been pretty badly done over. Looking down my body, it seemed as if at least half of it was in plaster cast. There was a machine on my left beeping and it appeared I was wired up to it. The bed was rock solid and I was tucked really tight into the sheets so I could barely move, not that movement was a good idea, given my state.

It turned out that someone at the party had taken offence to Jen and I and had phoned him up. He too was out and was drunk, but as soon as he found out that Jen was with someone else, rage took over and he got straight in his car and sped down the A2 to Canterbury. Had my mates not have pulled him off; they don't know what would have happened to me. No-one knows what happened to Jen apart from the fact she took a punch from him as he bundled her out of the door and into his Escort XR3i.

On seeing that I was unconscious and the amount of blood, my mates drove me to St. George's Hospital which luckily was about 5 minutes away. My Mum was called and came straight over. Bobby would be coming on the first train in the morning.

It was a perplexing situation. I felt lucky in a way, because I was in the wrong and it could have been worse. You hear quite regularly about crimes of passion and I know full well it was an incredibly dangerous game I was playing. I didn't even really feel anger towards Jen's boyfriend. It was a shame it couldn't have been a fair fight but I don't really think the guy was too worried about that.

However, someone grassed which is something that shouldn't really happen. Like I said, a majority of students here are from London and the surrounding areas and those were not the codes people adhered too. Plus, everyone was messing about at uni. Drugs, drinking, unprotected sex, casual relationships. Granted, not everyone was cheating, but for someone to be cold and calculated and make that call shows that they must have really wanted to make a point. It was unlike anyone I knew to do this. Also, it had to be someone Jen knew well as how else would they have this guy's contact number? The person culpable must be relatively easy to track down. I hoped my boys were already onto it, as getting beaten to a pulp was not really my idea of fun.

My mother wept by my bedside for what seemed like an eternity. I didn't know what to say so I kept repeating over and over again that I would be all right and it's ok. She held my hand so tight that it hurt me. I didn't stop her though, I just kept telling her it would be fine. She shook her head and looked up at me and said,

"You are just like your father, do you know that?"

I looked away and closed my eyes. I had never thought of it but I guess I was.

"You need to change before it's too late."

I was too proud, young and stupid to listen to her but she was right as I was headed for a very big fall.

Two months had passed and life was ticking by fantastically for Charlie and Jo. Jo had made sweeping changes to Charlie's flat and his lifestyle continued to become healthier as time went by. He was virtually domesticated! He ate his five a day (well three realistically), he was getting himself back to the gym and was sleeping a lot better. He had the occasional dabble recreationally but on the whole he felt less dependent on chemicals or maybe his dependency had changed from a chemical one to a human one.

He was serious about Jo and despite his early doubts (largely caused by Helen), he had never been happier. Jo was someone he felt would be very happy with. She was so calm and cool with people that she made life look so easy. She breezed through it with charm and elegance and although there was a certain charm to Charlie, on the inside he found life a struggle. Well that was before the good times began to roll.

Christmas loomed large on the horizon. Charlie and Jo couldn't wait. The first Christmas as a 'proper couple' in their own home seemed like a dream for them both. Being young and living in London didn't guarantee you a home at all. Most of Charlie and Jo's friends were pushing 30 and living with their parents. So in the grand scheme of things they were doing well for themselves. More importantly for the pair, Helen had not reared her ugly head again. Well that was not technically true. Charlie and Jo both made the decision to change their mobile phone numbers as a precaution. Four nights passed in Mid-November where Helen texted Charlie repeatedly. As he bedded down with the woman he loved, a ghost from the past came back to steal their happiness away. Since then however, no word had been sent from her.

Jo had an amazing Christmas gift planned for Charlie. She wanted to really show him how much he meant to her and had bought a flat screen TV with surround sound and the works. She couldn't wait to see his face on Christmas morning as he opened it! God knows what he will get me she thought. It didn't matter though, having each other was the most important thing for both of them.

"The pub crawl goes ahead as planned again this year, hun if you want to come?"

"On Christmas Eve?"

"Yep – I checked the trains and I can be back in Sutton by 10.30 pm-ish. I'll have to get two trains but it saves the hassle of travelling back on Christmas morning."

"You better be back here by then! Don't think you won't be with me on Christmas morning!" she said, half-joking, half not.

Charlie chuckled, "Of course I'll be back!"

The Christmas Eve pub crawl was an annual event that took place in Dartford. It was created and conceived by one of Charlie's best mates from school, Chris. It started in Crayford at the Bear and Ragged staff and weaved its way to the trashy dive that is Zen's in the heart of Dartford. The thing was, it began at 10.50am, 'with a knock on the door of the Bear' and it went on until past 2am normally. In the interests of preservation, Charlie was going to finish up by about half eight. Not that a nine hour session was not a heavy day, but at the moment he had something to go home for, something pulling him back.

It was over eight weeks before I was released from hospital. I missed loads of work which I would need to catch up, but, all in all, I was very happy about my first taste of freedom for a long while. I walked the route home as it wasn't far and I was looking forward to the fresh air. The roads were quiet and the sun rose and melted over the tiled rooftops and chimney stacks that make up the East side of this beautiful city.

I walked through the door which was unlocked as usual and saw all the guys in the front room sitting around. I could tell Brad was stoned already, he had a bleary look to him and this made me chuckle to myself.

My friends greeted me with a cold beer and a hug; I was pretty touched by the effort, as it was only about 9 in the morning. Ben wasn't around though for some reason, maybe he went to lectures. We sat around and talked quite openly about what happened. It turns out no-one really knew who told Mark (her boyfriend) about Jen and I. In fact the gossip itself was fairly limited. Jen had apparently run back into his arms and wasn't seen at uni for at least two weeks. She has denounced our 'affair' and I was most certainly persona non-grata at present. What a surprise. Anyway there were plenty more fish in the sea and even though I still felt a bit woozy from the painkillers, I felt a spliff was in order.

Brad thought it was the best idea he had heard in the last fifteen minutes and decided to skin up. The rest of us sat back and enjoyed the wonderful haze of university life.

9

The pub crawl was pretty much the first date written into our social calendar each year. People who hadn't seen each other since the last one made a real effort to get there and it was an exciting day out. Charlie enjoyed all of these things but also the fact that plenty of drugs would be floating around on the day. He also liked the fact it flew in the face of sobriety and plundered the importance of the majority's 'most important day of the year'.

Jo decided, as a gesture of good will, to drive Charlie the 40 or so miles around the M25 to the meet up. She was very welcome to attend but had plans with her friends in Sutton. As they had embraced before, Charlie leapt out of the car and into a world of hedonism. All at once he felt like a very lucky man.

The key players on the crawl generally met up nice and early around 10.45am to get in for first pints. It made the boys feel special that they were the first out and they exchanged maps of the route, wraps of coke prepared especially for the day and tall tales of what they had been up to over the past year. There was a sense of fulfilment and camaraderie as the cold icy air was broken with the warm bonhomie of a band of brothers anticipating the day ahead.

As the day passed, the conversation ebbed and flowed between trips to Australia, Thailand, the Balearics and Greece with much emphasis on exaggeration within the stories. But today we didn't care between the truth and fact, what was real and what was not, we were just glad to be together and celebrating, our way.

The day rolled into night as we took the well trodden path into Dartford Town, past the old school and church, where many a story was imparted about our lives growing up here. Charlie remembered with his old pal Steve, how he was chased by gangs and had to hide in the grounds of the church, keeping his breathing low and his body still as the gang slowly gave up the chase. Chris regaled us with how they used to play 'knock down ginger' at the school housing and waited to see which of their teachers they could disturb. Charlie remembered cordoning off the whole of West Hill with traffic cones that he and his pals found lying around. They hid and watched as car after car waited bemused at the situation, before eventually moving the cones and driving through only for Charlie and his pals to cordon off the other side for the journey home. It was all silly, childish stuff but the reminiscing passed the time beautifully between pubs and bars, as they made their way into town.

Charlie and the others found their way to The Crown, the first stop in Dartford town centre. Time was pressing on for Charlie and it looked unlikely he would be able to make the Courthouse this time around, so he made the most of the time, by hoofing two hefty lines with Steve in a cubicle in the pub. It was risky business as the pub tonight was getting busier and you knew people were itching to get in the cubicle, probably for the same reason they were. So they chopped their lines wide and in an amateurish manner, which was never as smooth a ride as when you had time to chop up the powder, nice and fine. Oh well, needs must, Charlie thought.

They dived out as they always did, one after the other, paying no attention to other punters around them. Most people knew what they were doing and didn't have the bottle to say or do anything, others just didn't care. They tidied up their faces and headed back into the chaos as the feeling of euphoria seeped into their veins.

The boys drank heartily and rapidly, the coke sank in and always sped up the drinking pace. One of the main side effects of the gear was that you never reached that cut off point that you do when you're not high. You feel invincible and can keep going and going, without the need to stop. This was dangerous, Charlie had thought in times gone by, but tonight he ceased to care.

Time had passed by and it was time for Charlie to make his way to the station. He was pleased to be going back to Sutton despite the incredible day he'd had. He looked forward to seeing Jo out with her mates. He looked forward to walking into the club and being lavished with compliments and attention as girls always seemed to do with him.

He said his goodbyes and left on his own, where the true effects of the gear really kicked in. They always said that when you were with likeminded people, you never felt as wasted, but now he was on his own, he felt like he was floating down the street, as if his feet were nowhere near the ground. At first there was a wave of paranoia but as he boarded the train and put on his iPod he calmed down and felt better. His music sounded incredible every note resonated in his eardrum, every chord petrified and wailed as if it was the first time he had heard it. He closed his eyes and drifted off into bliss…

Steve left Charlie at the bottom of Dartford station near the Orchard. Steve was going to pay a visit to one of their old haunts, The Paper Moon, where they used to drink as Dartford Grammar sixth form students. Having taken one look inside as he reached the door, he decided against it. It was and had remained the Dartford Grammar School sixth form pub. He weighed up his options and headed out into the town centre. He thought it best to go back and join some of the guys he knew back in the Courthouse.

He sidled in the back way and, as he opened the double doors, the warmth hit him and immediately caused him to flush. He clearly hadn't realised how cold he was as he was pretty buzzing. He got in, greeted his mates and went to the bar to order some drinks. As he was waiting he heard behind him a familiar voice.

"Hi Steve. How are you?" He flipped around to see Helen, dressed to the nines and made up far too heavily.

"Hi Helen, yeah pretty fucked, y'know , it's been a long day."

"I bet. What time did you start?"

"Well, I got down to town about midday. The other boys had already started…"

"Where are the other boys, Steve? Where is Charlie? I haven't seen him."

Steve's heart sank in this moment. He knew about how psychopathic this girl could be. He had seen it first hand with Charlie over the last five years.

Steve hesitated, "He…uh…I think he has gone home…back to Sutton…"

"Why? When did he go?" She barked abruptly. Her face changed and you could see a dark cloud descend over the two of them. The pleasantries had passed as Helen realised she wouldn't see Charlie tonight.

"He has just got the train. I walked up to the station…"

"But he never leaves early, he always is out. I don't understand why he…"

Then she realised. Something she had been keeping deep down inside and prayed was not true.

"He has, hasn't he? He's got a fucking girlfriend hasn't he?" At this point she was shouting and beginning to lose any remaining composure she had. She was drawing a crowd.

Steve not being one to like scenes, especially with women and not really knowing what to say, opted for the truth, thinking in the long term it would be the best option. Unfortunately, he bypassed the effect in the short term.

"Well…I think he may have gone back to see someone…yes…"

Steve knew full well the extent of things between Charlie and Jo, but wanted to cover for Charlie as much as he could.

"I fucking knew it!" And as the realisation she had been warding off, seeped into her consciousness, she smashed her glass down on the bar and felt it crack in her hand and splinter into many pieces.

Helen proceeded to push Steve and try to hit him, but even in his inebriated state, he managed to hold her off before one of her best mates, Laura, grabbed her and dragged her to the upstairs girls bathroom.

Steve was angry at the incident. He felt it was not something he should have to deal with. He was embarrassed in front of his mates and tended to steer clear from his friend's ex-girlfriends for precisely this reason. He turned to his mates and tried to wipe this horror show from his mind, before going to have a cheeky line and a piss in the toilet.

To get up to either toilet, there was a double door you had to pass through, which led to the stairs. Halfway up the stairs a large mirror hung and in it, he noticed Helen's icy gaze boring into him through the glass. Before he had time to react, Helen had jumped off from the top stair she was sitting on and had launched her stiletto at Steve's head. As Steve ducked, the shoe smashed into the mirror with such force that it splintered and cracked with a large boom and dropped into tiny pieces on the floor. This alerted the mainstay of the Courthouse drinking faithful and many of them helped to drag an inconsolable, uncontrollable woman away and out into the cold, harsh night. Steve once again couldn't make sense of his feelings. He was angry at Charlie, but mostly with Helen at her inability to cope with life and what it throws at you. He was overwhelmed too, by a feeling of utter sadness and despair as he watched a sweet, young girl descend deeper into chaos and madness. She had everything she had wanted; a boyfriend, a job, a place to live. Here she was, having lost everything and on Christmas Eve of all nights, she was being dragged out of a pub by her feet and hands by friends and strangers alike, with no answer or remedy.

Why wasn't Charlie here? It was his fault this was happening, the fucking prick should be dealing with this himself!

Charlie drifted in and out of consciousness peacefully and serenely until his phone rang and he saw it was Steve.

"Mate you're not going to fucking believe what has happened…"

And as the story unfolded, Charlie could sense a bitter and accusatory tone in Steve's voice. He had heard it before. He knew his day and night had gone too well for him just to roll back home happily.

"Mate I'm sorry, that's fucked up. She is mad, fucking mad! You shouldn't have to deal with it." Charlie tried to dissipate the situation.

"Yeah, well, I did mate and she knows about Jo now. That's what set her off! I am serious, she could have had my eye out!"

"Well sorry, what can I say? Listen mate, I got to go see you later."

"All right, see you."

As the phone went dead, Charlie pondered the situation and although he could understand that his predicament had taken a turn for the worse, he felt as if he was far away from anything. Being in transit and the effects of the drugs made him feel blasé and able to cope. Charlie even afforded himself a little smile as he imagined Steve, one of his least athletic friends, trying to dodge a speeding stiletto!

Either way, Charlie had a new life now, away from that and was determined to make it work.

He got off at London Bridge station and walked down the platform. It was largely deserted. Most people were indoors or out in the pubs and bars gearing up for the festive celebration. In another time or place, Charlie thought about feeling really displaced and insecure as he imagined a nation of people with their loved ones, as he stumbled down the ramp in the centre of a desolate city. But he imagined Jo drinking her amaretto and apple juice, chatting to her friends or on the dance floor and he felt an enormous sense of well being.

As time passed by I felt better about my injuries and what had happened to me. I felt a sense of guilt really, knowing that most guys who had a girlfriend, would have done exactly the same as Mark, Jen's boyfriend did. I knew I deserved it, but still was concerned about knowing who the person that made that call was. And why? It just seemed at the end of a party, where we were all leathered, it was a bizarre thing to do. No-one had any connections with him, apart from Jen obviously, so who would be bothered to make that call?

As I walked out of the kitchen, I saw Brad sneak down the stairs and out of the house.

"Hey, where are you going?"

"Oh, hey man, just got to pop out for some smokes and stuff."

"Ok, see you in a bit."

With that, Brad shut the door and I didn't see him again for two days.

The night had passed well and Jo came to at about 9.15am. She rolled over to hug her man on Christmas morning, with a grin on her face, to find a cold empty space and Charlie, not there. She rubbed her eyes and heard the muffled sound of talking through the wall. It was Charlie on the landline.

She opened the bedroom door quietly and listened to the conversation…

"No, it's not any of your business!"

"Of course not. For fuck's sake it's Christmas morning! I won't speak to you again now, this is it!"

"Maybe she is. It has fuck all to do with you."

Jo heard the conversation end and she sidled back to bed. She pretended to sleep as Charlie clattered around in the front room, clearly perturbed.

Jo decided to get up; it was Christmas day after all. She walked into the front room and Charlie whizzed around.

"Merry Christmas honey!" He sounded forced, anxious.

Jo immediately burst into tears. She knew he was talking to that bitch and on Christmas morning! Their first Christmas together! She was livid, she had managed to infect Christmas, with her bullshit and whining.

"I can't believe you were speaking to her on Christmas day. You prick, you…" she blurted out.

Charlie grabbed her and held her as she sobbed into his arms.

Brad left on a Sunday morning and didn't arrive back until Tuesday afternoon. Once again he entered quietly, while Ben and I were sitting in the front room, watching a film. We hardly heard the door open nor the padding up the stairs. It was like he was a ghost. But we had missed him and been worried about where he was. Brad was a homebody, if he wasn't in his room smoking weed and playing guitar, then he was downstairs smoking weed and watching TV or playing playstation.

I looked at Ben and we both decided to head upstairs to see what was going on. We found Brad's door wedged shut. We looked at each other and Ben decided to knock. There was no answer. We knocked again and there was no answer still. We decided to go in, worried in case he was in trouble so we barged the door open. Inside we found nothing, no sign of Brad, just a tidy room with a window left open.

As we came out of the room confused and perplexed, I gave a cursory glance into my own room and saw Brad sitting on my bed staring up at both of us. I tapped Ben's arm and he breathed in quickly.

"Hey, Brad. Where have you been? We texted you, we were worried."

Brad didn't break his glance from me. He got up, walked out of my room and past us, into his own room. He slammed the door and locked it behind him.

Christmas day, in fact the Christmas period, passed remarkably well for Charlie and Jo. Despite the overarching shadow of Helen being ever-present, they moved on and refused to let her madness affect them, or their future.

As it was, they had booked a weekend away with some friends to Inverness for New Year's Eve. It felt nice to get away given all that had happened and the future felt bright.

Helen had finally seemed to admit that the relationship with Charlie was over and with a little passing time, they felt she would be gone from their lives forever. This of course was the dream state and not the reality, although landing at Glasgow airport amidst the cold and fog; they felt isolated, but completely together, a refreshing feeling.

The couple hired a car, a Renault Megane and despite Charlie's initial reticence, he enjoyed driving it. He remembered his Father's distrust and dislike of French cars (which probably at the time was founded), but realised now most new cars, were of a pretty good standard. It was easy to drive and fairly nippy so he couldn't complain.

They wound their way up the 200 mile trip north on the 'A' roads of Scotland, appreciating the scenic views and in some respects, the wintry chill. The greatest thing about being in the deep midwinter is getting indoors, cosy and warm and they most certainly were.

The trip to Inverness was dry which made conditions easy to handle and for the most part they admired the countries beautiful hills, valleys and villages. Most houses were lit up brightly for the Christmas holidays, adding to the great beauty and feel of where they were.

Charlie reminisced through Scottish history, or at least the one in his mind, thinking of great battles, proud men and the valiant actions of a nation of underdogs. He knew as well that most of his education was either untrue or elaborated, but at that moment he cared not a bit, happy to throw himself into his fantasies forthwith.

The smoking ban had been introduced in Scotland and it really had an impact. It was heart-warming to see the pubs in Inverness overflowing with people, a truly festive scene, (when really it was just smokers, gagging for a drag.) The good news for Charlie was that he would not be one of them, as in the most part he had given up and while he was with Jo, he certainly wasn't going to be seen smoking.

The house became stranger and stranger as the weeks drifted by in a wintry haze. The grey and despondent gloom outside, mirrored the collective feeling in the house. I was spending a lot of time in my room or at the college trying to study (yes, study) just because it was a better atmosphere than being at home. Brad had become more and more isolated from us. He either commandeered the front room or was frosty and never came out of his room. His answers had become largely monosyllabic and it was hard work just being in the same house as him.

He also kept around this new guy he'd met, who we couldn't relate to at all. He used to be a smoking friend for Brad, but now he was around far more often, the hanger-on we called him. He was always where Brad was and having a virtual stranger constantly in the house made life difficult.

Ben was rarely around the house either. He had become distant in a different way. Whenever I saw him he was always really happy to see me and saying we should go out for beers and so on together, but he never really seemed to want to. It was all talk, for show. He seemed to have another crowd he was hanging around with; at least I assumed it was a crowd because he wasn't knocking around with us anymore. I tried to reach Brad and get him out of the house for beers and so on but it was a lost cause. He had literally gone up in smoke and seemed unreachable now.

10

The months rolled on and Charlie and Jo had another trip planned, this time to France, in celebration of Jo's Mum and Dad's 25th Wedding anniversary. They were going to stay in the same hotel they were married in all of those years ago. The best thing for Charlie and Jo was that it was a freebie and promised to be a fairly enjoyable event. Charlie also had plans to make this an unforgettable weekend for all involved. He wanted to propose and was pretty certain that Jo would say yes. She hadn't as much as dropped hints to him, but he knew that their love affair was something special and she was smitten. Plus, all girls are secretly desperate to get married. Jo was a white wedding kind of girl and she knew that when the time came her Dad would want to let her have all that she would want on the day.

Charlie was a traditionalist of sorts and desired to ask her father for Jo's hand in marriage. He knew Jo's Dad would appreciate that and he felt quite strongly about doing the right thing.

They were staying in Brittany for three nights and Charlie had only this time to get everything in place that he wanted to. Obviously, one of the days was entirely devoted to her parents' party, so he knew he had to act fast to make his plan work. They arrived in the late afternoon and took some time in their room to make love and relax before heading out to the coast to enjoy a meal in the evening. Charlie planned to ask Jim the following morning, at breakfast, and he was becoming more and more nervous as time wore on. He also had to get Jo out of the way long enough to speak to Jim which was a tough enough task in itself. Anyway, Charlie planned to enjoy the fresh seafood and the sea air that evening and not worry about it until later. After all, he wouldn't want his wife to be to get any idea about his plan.

Charlie slept soundly that night and woke up feeling excited and nervous. He went to breakfast and ate heartily. The butter croissants and the coffee went down well and as they wrapped up their meal, Jo was rushing Charlie to try and get back to the room and get ready. It was essentially a day of preparation before the big party the next day and in between visiting relatives, there would be a lot of running around to do.

Charlie accepted Jo's eyes motioning him away from the table. He looked at her and smiled and whispered he would be up in a minute. Jo harrumphed and plonked herself back in her seat. Charlie panicked and whispered for her to go to the room and he would be up in a second. She looked at him with a little bit of annoyance; a bright girl not being able to comprehend what on earth this silly man was doing. She eventually left, saying her goodbyes to the family and agreeing to meet in an hour or so in reception, to head out to the hypermarket.

Charlie sat opposite Jo's parents. They look perplexed yet interested as Jim tucked hastily into another butter croissant.

"I, ah, wanted to speak to you…" this clearly caused some initial worry as like most parents they assume something is wrong.

"Yes, Charlie what is it?"

"I know this may be a shock, given time and everything but…I…"

Charlie was so nervous. He was usually calm, collected and in control in these sort of situations. He was able to blag parents and make them feel comfortable and happy, but all his previous skills seemed to elude him at this juncture.

"I would like to ask you, Jim, if I can marry your daughter…"

I was so sick of all the problems with the house I had really decided to throw myself back into my studies and have my face seen at university as much as possible. It was a fairly long walk to the college, to the end of Zealand Road (which sounded plenty more exotic than it was. Essentially a road of ex-council houses filled with students) across and over the railway bridge near the station. The pathway from the station led through to a pretty Kentish road with small terraced houses on either side and followed directly towards town and the Cross Keys pub.

I trod the road quietly and slowly towards the university, past the supermarket and Blockbuster and towards the University City wall. It was here you had the choice of going left or right and taking the main entrance to the uni near the cathedral or going right and taking the rear gate. We generally always took the left road, largely because it passed the legendary Jaspers pizza restaurant. This was one of the few places that was open at 2.30am after the clubs had kicked out. It was also infamous for its chilli pizza, which partakers would know about for a few days after consumption.

Today, I decided to take the right turn. Events seemed a little topsy-turvy and had I* had a companion, I may well have gone the other way, regaling stories about drunken antics over a slice of pizza. However things were not as they should be and I fancied a change of scenery.

As I walked past the roundabout, I noticed that this way was actually quite pleasant. The trees were bare, or had a few green leaves on them. There were pretty little Georgian houses along the right-hand side of the road, whilst the stone wall and various older university buildings ran along the left-hand side. There was a red post box and an altogether English feel, and I was buoyed and warmed by the surroundings. I realised all moments were fleeting and even the limbo I seemed to be faced with now would pass in time.

"Hey, how is it going? What you been up to?"

It was Dan, a friend from the rugby team who had just come out of college. I stopped to talk to him, despite being five minutes late for my lecture.

"Hello mate! All good. It's been quite quiet recently though, just trying to keep my head down and get in here occasionally!"

"Yeah, I know what you mean. It is a struggle though. I have done two lectures so calling it a day. You know we are having a few beers over at our house tonight before going up to the Tenet if you fancy popping over. We haven't had a session for a while so thought it was about time. Join us if you fancy?"

"Cool that would be nice, our house is a bit...dead...at the moment." I tentatively added.

Dan looked around nervously. It seemed he was trying to continue the conversation. I didn't know why he was, as I was quite ready to leave it there.

"Yeah, I see, how is Brad? I haven't seen him around for a while."

"He is doing his own thing, smoking, smoking, smoking."

"Ha! He does love all that doesn't he?" Dan looked over his shoulder and rubbed his hands together. Why was he panicky?

"Look Dan I have got to get in, otherwise I will be la..."

"How's your better half pal? I haven't seen her for a while?" He blurted.

It was then over Dan's shoulder, I saw something instantly drawing me nearer, something I knew all too well. Just behind the back wall of the college, I saw a glimpse of long blonde hair and a voice I knew all too well. Jen.

I looked at Dan and he visibly slumped. The prick-he was clearly trying to hold me up. I stormed on up towards the college, intrigued by what might be behind the wall. I moved around to see her full, feminine figure underneath a tree and the figures of two men. I didn't wish to reveal myself, so I jogged up to the nearside wall and snuck up as close as I could. Jen was looking around and she was being spoken to by another guy. He was holding her hand...no...he was taking something from her...it seemed to be a package but they were also smiling and kissing as they swapped something in their hands.

Jen gazed up adoringly at the guy she was holding and she beamed a broad smile as they moved out of embrace. She walked slowly away from the boy who turned and put something into his jeans pocket. As he did this, he looked around suspiciously and my heart sank as I pushed myself up against the wall and jogged away from the college and out of the back gates, away from what I had seen.

Had I just seen what I thought? The face seemed so familiar? *Could it be?*

I ran up the road to a phone box and went in. I pulled the receiver off the hook. My hands were shaking with fear, panic and adrenaline. I waited for the boy to come out of the gates. He looked one way and then looked straight towards me in the phone box, like an idiot pretending to be making a call. Who makes calls from phone boxes anymore anyway?

As the boy gazed at me, my heart sank and my body fell against the hard glass. It was Ben. As I watched him walk away, back towards town, I couldn't bring myself to leave the box. I was shaken and angry. I couldn't fathom what the hell was going on? I finally summoned the strength to leave and push myself into the cold, winter air. As I did I heard the sound of a car behind, coming towards me along the road. As I sped up along the pavement, the car seemed to slow to a halt and the engine turned off. I felt frightened, not knowing what on earth was going on and my imagination playing tricks on me. I sped up to a brisk walk until I reached the corner of the road where the roundabout was and turned around. There it was, the XR3i. As I focused my eyes in on the car, I noticed that there was no-one inside. I stayed where I was, eyes locked on the vehicle, perplexed. I didn't hear the doors go. No-one got out I was sure. I turned to make the long, cold walk home confused and upset, when behind me the engine started again.

11

On a warm summer's day in the West of France, as the leaves on the trees rustled in the midmorning wind and folks ate heartily in a cosy breakfast room, Jim Turner agreed to give away his daughter.

It was a massive relief for Charlie, although he felt what was meant to be would be, regardless of his answer. But luckily for him, Jim snapped up Charlie's hand and agreed to the marriage instantly.

This all led to the rather enjoyable task of acquiring champagne, flowers and gifts, which of course, had to be done before the evening, when Charlie planned to make his proposition. As he made his way back to the room, he was struggling to manage his glee. Despite this he was focused and this made his outward demeanour somewhat perplexing to Jo, who was concerned about why her boyfriend was behaving bizarrely.

During the day, whilst Jim and Charlie skulked off to collect a few bits and bobs, Jo became more and more perturbed, especially since her Father was now joining in the strange acts of her other half. Anyway, Jo was dragged around jewellery shops and the like by her mother, playing her role and keeping her out of the way, while the boys grabbed the necessaries.

Once the day was done there were a few moments for the lovers to be alone in their room before the evening saw a trip to Cancale for a meal. It was here Charlie would ask Jo for her hand. The family had a huge dinner date with friends and other relatives and it was organised for the two youngsters to go to a separate restaurant. The area was new to Charlie who had only explored France on a limited scale. He had been to Paris a few times with previous lovers and had travelled to the South with his family when he was a boy, but Brittany was new to him. Thus he was pleased to find the location and vistas nothing short of spectacular. The beach left a bit to be desired. However, the restaurants were situated in a square by the coast and as the sun set slowly in the west, it bathed the seafront in a red-orange glow.

Things came to a head with the pair as they were eating, when Jo broke down in tears at the table. She claimed that she had felt weird all day because everyone around her had not been themselves. She was right, to be fair, and Charlie had a real task on his hands calming her down and getting her in the right frame of mind! After the meal, they went and had a few drinks in a café next door. It was strangely refreshing as Charlie was always used to the respectable, touristy watering holes of Paris. Yet, this place had a real working class feel to it. There were drunkards lounging over the bar, old hags laughing a little too loudly, men filling up their glasses far too quickly. Charlie liked it. If he closed his eyes and listened he felt he could be back in the Wetherspoons in Blighty.

Once Jo was back to her bubbly self, Charlie invited her out for a walk along the seafront where he hoped to ask the question. He was a little bit frustrated at himself as he had dithered quite a lot. He knew he could have asked her on a few occasions but his bravery had deserted him. It reminded him of times when he was younger, when he was trying to make a move on girls and ask them out. Yet he rarely had the bottle to pop the question or move in for the kiss, scared stiff of the rejection. However, here he was. A boy again, staring that rejection square in the face, wondering what the answer would be. As they walked along the seafront promenade, Jo was excited once more, this time about a holiday they had planned for next summer, to the West of America. Charlie in a sly and underhanded way saw his chance to finally get it out.

"I am not sure we are going to be able to go to America next year Jo." He said with mock solemnity.

Jo looked upset and asked him why, screwing up her face like a little girl confused, like when her father told her 'no' as a child.

"Well because…Charlie dropped to one knee…I had really hoped you would marry me instead…"

The car rolled forward and I saw the two figures in the front, Jen and her boyfriend. I hastily turned around and continued walking towards the town inevitably on my way home. I knew they must have seen me and were clearly trying to avoid me. So why start the car up and drive right past me?

As they went past, both of them looked dead ahead as if they had not noticed me at all. What will happen when they see Ben? Presumably blank him also. Jen wouldn't want her 'other half' to know about her new plaything I guessed. What a fucking bitch, I thought. She knew how much I wanted her and she left me in the lurch, after taking a pasting from her old man. On top of that, she seems to be fucking one of my best pals. Well, ex best pals. Maybe I should go and grass Ben up to this prick and see how he likes hospital food. No, that was not the answer. Ben for all his sins was still a mate and mates *should* be loyal. As the car moved towards the traffic lights, it slowed and pulled in. A figure emerged from the garages behind Blockbuster and slid into the backseat. I knew without even looking that it would be Ben. My heart skipped again as I tried to make sense of what the fuck was going on.

They sped off at the lights towards home which seemed to be where they must be going. Jen didn't live this far east and the boyfriend was a long way from his home. That's where I was going to head then. I started running down the street and over the lights to get home as quickly as possible and try and find out what on earth was going on. My anger was rising and the blood pumped through my veins powering my limbs faster and faster. I made it over the bridge, past the old person's house on the corner of Zealand Road, where the decrepit cat perched on the window sill and eyed me with derision. *Fuck it,* I thought. *Fuck all of them.* As I turned the corner into my road I looked up ahead at my house and lo and behold outside was parked an old Ford Escort XR3i. Here goes, I thought.

Jo accepted Charlie's proposition instantly and the two embraced passionately together in the warm evening air. It was one of the many moments that they would have together where they both were completely satisfied in each other's arms.

I walked up to the house and opened the front door loudly. I had nothing to be afraid or ashamed of in this instance and I wanted some answers. There was rustling coming from upstairs, but before I had a chance, something hit me hard in the side of the face.

"You again, you prick!" It was Jen's boyfriend, but this time he hadn't caught me quite as unaware as he did last time. I steadied myself swiftly and tackled him into the living room, smashing his back into the fire place. We grappled for a while before I eventually got the better of him and hit him a few times in the head and in the kidney. I managed to stand up and what my Father would call 'the red mist' came over me as I laid into him with my fists until his face was covered in blood.

There was a pounding of feet down the stairs and I felt someone throw me off and onto the sofa. Brad stood in front of me, his eyes raging as he looked down at me. Jen burst into the room and ran to her boyfriend crying and spluttering. She tried to jump on me scratching at me, but Brad and I threw her off.

She kept saying over again, "you don't understand, you don't know what you're doing!" She repeated and repeated until I finally bawled out, "well explain it to me then! What the fuck is going on!"

She curled up into a ball on the sofa and whimpered the words, "you wouldn't understand."

I tried to reach her. In a way I loved her and still wanted to be by her side, so pushing Brad out the way I went to her and held her hand.

"Explain it to me Jen. What is the secret? I want to help you!" I tried to empathise, searching her big lost eyes for an answer, anything to shed some light.

She just stared at me blankly and sobbed away. I looked down at her man and saw him smirk at me through the blood on his face. For good measure, I gave him another dig to the jaw and he quietened down again.

At the doorway to the living room emerged Ben who saw the mess I had made of his new pal and Jen sobbing away. He looked at her then looked at me. He weighed something up and then made a charge for me, swearing and lashing out. My hands were sore and I was feeling torn out from inside. The last thing I wanted was another fight, but before I had the chance to steel myself, Brad stood in Ben's way took his weight and drove him back against the window.

"No mate, I don't think so. Not this time!" He shouted.

"Fuck off, Brad. Get out of my way." Ben retorted.

"No. It's your entire fault this mess. Thanks to you and her."

"Leave her out of it Brad. It has nothing to do with you, you fucking skaghead, if it weren't for us you would have been clucking the last few weeks. I want that cunt!" Ben screamed. *Skaghead?* I really was out of the loop here.

"That stops now!" cried Brad. "You fucking set Charlie up. I know what the plan is, I have seen Jen's diary, I have seen the receipts, I know your fucking plan, you cunt!"

Ben's face dropped and Jen stopped her crying and moved towards Brad.

"You don't understand, we love each other it's got to…Jen tell him…"

Ben was reaching and the worm was beginning to turn.

"No. She is a fucked up bitch. You fucked Charlie over when he was with her. He is your pal and you fucked him, for that fucking skank! It's no good Ben, what you have done." Brad retorted.

"But…"

Jen was wiping the blood from her boyfriend's face and he stirred, angered by the words he was hearing.

"You made the phone call to this prick, that night didn't you Ben? Because you were jealous! You wanted her and the shit he was selling and you fucked our mate over for it."

Ben was speechless and embarrassed. He tried to muster words but none came. His shoulders slumped and in one last futile effort, he lunged at Brad. I quickly leapt up and helped Brad wrestle him to the floor, where he remained and broke down into tears.

Brad and I looked at each other and without thinking I gave him the most almighty hug. I had felt out in the cold over the past few months and it was so nice to have a friend back and have some questions answered. Mostly, I missed my pal. We went in and sat down, listening to Jen apologise over and over again in the living room. She was getting hysterical to such an extent; we didn't even hear the sirens and the police knocking on the front door.

12

Jo's parents' party passed without a hitch. There was even some time to introduce formally to the awaiting crowd, the fact that Jo had become betrothed. Everyone was happy and as so happens on holiday the problems awaiting you in your own country, seem far away and never to return. After the party, Jo, Charlie and her brother Tim went to the late night bar to continue their celebrations. Jo drank champagne, while the boys drunk whiskey and smoked cigars. It was a brilliant time for the Turner family. Charlie, of course, was a very happy man also. He felt like a chapter of sadness and longing was over in his life and he had bagged, or at least was one step closer, to bagging a girl he was really happy with.

So the break was a complete success. They left Brittany and made their way to the ferry as a tight knit unit. The wedding was planned for the following summer, which gave them a year and a few months to plan it and get it right. Jo as well did not want things by halves; she wanted the perfect summer wedding. But they were betrothed and at this moment in time, that was all that mattered to them.

I found out well after the fight in my house, that I was taken into custody on a Thursday. I was let out, for want of a better word, on Saturday morning at 7.34am. It turns out that the police were called by the neighbours after they had heard raised voices and violent sounds from next door. I have said before this was an ex-council road and the actions taking place in the house were, to be fair, nothing short of extraordinary. The walls were fairly thin and thus I have no qualms about the police being called.

Although what they found and the questioning that took place was nothing short of scandalous. I was searching for answers, but more for my well being rather than just for a nick which the police seemed to be adamant to get.

I was let out with a caution, presumably for my aggression and essentially ABH which had been committed on Mark. Unsurprisingly, he declined to press charges given our history and took his rap on the chin. He was found with a substantial amount of heroin upon his person as well as a large supply of morphine. After the police had heard Jen's, mine and Ben's testimony, they decided to prosecute him with the intent to supply to others and he remains in police custody and probably won't be out for a long, long while.

Jen left a few hours before me after spilling her beans, which until now I had no idea about and in all honestly was quite a shock to the system. She left largely unscathed legally, but we had unfinished business.

Ben, however, was charged with intent to cause ABH and possession of a class 'A' substance with intent to supply. This made me feel rather sickened as despite this episode he was a pal who I felt for. The police though had no remorse and found a rather large package of heroin in his back pocket and were under the impression he had intent to supply. The fact that I had witnessed him take this off Jen, I kept to myself and probably will do to my dying day.

Brad was let out on Friday. Luckily he wasn't drug tested because that might have been a problem for him. It turns out that for over three months he had been supplied heroin by Jen and her other half, but as the story unfolded in the Canterbury Constabulary, he was correctly deemed in the right in this instance and he got what can only be termed as a 'get out of jail free' card.

I went home and met Brad. We had a long discussion about what had gone on and made some real plans to move forward. I found out a lot of things as well about the past few months. It turns out that it was Ben who made the phone call to Mark about Jen and I. Ben had been infatuated with her from the start of university, but he had never really made an impression on her. All the times he saw me with her made him more and more angry. He got to the point where he couldn't take it anymore and made that late night phone call. Mark thought something was up as her texts became more sporadic over the evening in question. As soon as he had the confirmation, he left for Canterbury.

Mark was a real horrible case from what we could work out. He was quite a big drug dealer from Grays in Essex, where he was from. Battering people was part of his business so he had no qualms about coming down and defending his honour.

To make matters more interesting, he was using Jen as a distributor for his stuff in Canterbury. To be fair it made sense. Canterbury, as much as it was a city, was a bit of a backwater and apart from the occasional bit of weed, many class 'A' drugs were pretty tricky to get hold of.

They started distributing a bit of speed and coke to the students that Jen knew and as time went on, he began trying to sell crack and heroin to the big smokers; Brad was one of them.

"Quite a bit before you and her got together she had approached me about trying something new. I always tried to ward her off, but as you know she can be quite persuasive," Brad declared.

"You two didn't…"

"No nothing like that happened, I wouldn't do that. I knew you were really into her. I thought you were going to dump Bobby for her at one stage."

"I don't think, with hindsight… she was really into me."

"Well, who knows? Anyway, she kept on and on about trying this stuff. She never called it brown or skag so it didn't really seem too bad. At one of the parties she gave me a small wrap of it and the tin foil and told us how to do it. We gave it a whirl and the rest of it…"

"What was it like?"

"Man, it was fucking incredible, but…you just can't stop once you've started. It's just so…still and calm…but I ended up getting too far gone and I couldn't control it. That's why I was out so much, trying to make money with Harry to get more."

"You didn't inject it?"

"No, no. We were close but…I stopped in time."

"How did you stop?"

"It just got too far. I was contemplating doing things that I would never have dreamed of, just to get the next hit. I was completely fucked."

"Have you got help to stop?"

"I spoke to someone at the college and they put me in touch with someone to talk to. Oh and of course I have been taking these morphine supplements!"

"Oh, I see!" I pondered what it might be like before asking, "Can I try one?"

"Man...it's not even 9am...oh, fuck it...why not? When they are gone they are gone though. That's it."

"Definitely. For old times' sake."

"Sweet."

With that, the whole nasty episode was over. Brad and I got high and I could see what he meant about the strength of the stuff. It was really good! After that we threw the rest away and had a beer and a spliff and continued to chat, quite possibly a load of rubbish, about music, friendship and the future.

PART 2

13

Time had never been particularly important to Charlie. He felt it was a manmade device for control and didn't pay too much attention to it unless he really had to. However, in the run up to the wedding it took on a different meaning completely. Charlie saw his life divided neatly into timeframes. How long he had to organise a venue, how long he had for the suits, the food and so on. This was beginning to burden him somewhat. On top of this, his love for Jo remained strong and he could see that she was beginning to strain under the pressure of the preparations.

The couple were lucky mind you, as Jim, who was a kindly and relaxed man, was very keen to fulfil his 'father of the bride' duties. He was a traditional man, a true Englishman, a dying breed perhaps and he was very pleased that Charlie proposed in the manner that he did. He wanted to entertain the guests at his daughter's wedding in a flourishing and exciting manner. With Charlie's creativity, Jo's perseverance and Jim's money, it was certain to be quite an event.

The date was set for August of the following year and the venue was in the pipeline. Things were moving forward but there did seem to be an awful amount of other bits and pieces to organise. The scale and magnitude of the event seemed to be spiralling out of the couple's control. However, they were well supported and loved by both families and thus as the going got particularly tough, Charlie organised a trip to Thailand; Jo having travelled and worked there before was more than keen for the break.

In addition to the organisation of the wedding, Charlie's father had become quite ill over the last few months. Charlie was particularly close to his Father and feared the worst for his health. He was a heavy smoker and initially he thought he had a chest infection that wouldn't shift. However, after a serious scare in the night, he was admitted to hospital with a tight chest and short breath. They had found a lump in his lung and it was obvious what the diagnosis was. He had responded well to the treatment, but Charlie was adamant he was going to stay with his father as he had done throughout his illness. But as the holiday grew nearer and nearer, Charlie's father insisted he went, saying something along the lines of 'you need to see the world son.'

Charlie was a natural born worrier and in his head he was panicking that this was the last time he would see his father alive. His father assured him that he would most definitely be here on Charlie's return and to 'fuck off and enjoy yourself!' So Charlie left, feeling a little bit guilty but in a way, somewhat relieved. He didn't realise the burden and weight he had been carrying for his family, but as soon as the plane took off, he felt some of his worry ebb away into the night sky.

Charlie had never been to this area of the world before and was immediately struck by the thick warmth of the air as he disembarked the aircraft. The horizon was awash with colour as the sun set lazily across the eastern sky. He watched the palm trees sway in the breeze and as was often the way with Charlie, he felt almost immediately at ease in his new surroundings. He put it down as one of god's little jokes. Y'know being unable to fit in and feel comfortable where he lived but as soon as he travelled to far away lands, he knew he was home.

This feeling was confirmed as they checked into the D and D inn on Khaosan Road. As soon as Charlie had dropped his bags and plonked himself on the bed, he had drifted off into a deep, deep slumber not to stir for the next 12 hours.

Jo seemed very happy and content with life at present. Yes, she had her worries and qualms about the future and of what it would hold. Mostly though, she believed she was in love and wanted to cling to that feeling as long as she could. She looked at her fiancée snoring on the bed and giggled to herself at how she found herself truly living her life after the year of to-ing and fro-ing with inadequate men over the past year or so.

First there was Jon. A boy she knew from when she was growing up around Croydon and used to see in Blue Orchid, a local nightclub, for years and years before. She never really fancied Jon but he was persistent and methodical in his pursuasion of her, that in the end she found it hard to turn him down. For instance, the evening before her first Thailand trip, he came to her door with a goodbye present and card. They had never had relations of any kind and this behaviour she found ultimately touching.

Upon her return, he would follow her when she went out, not in a menacing way, but in a desperate way, offering to walk her home and being the shoulder to cry on when her heart was left unrequited by her other lovers.

Jo eventually submitted one night when she was feeling hurt and unloved. Jon sent a text at the right time and she let her guard down and slept with him. It was never satisfying mind you, as Jo knew in her heart, she did not want him and, in a way, she was repaying him for the years of adoration. Not to mention, Jon's infatuation for the girl of his dreams, left him wanting in the bedroom and with this her contempt for him grew. Poor old Jon fell deeper and deeper in love with her and Jo felt sad for him as she knew he would never be the one. She thought back on that fateful night she met Charlie. She knew he was one of Jon's close friends and again felt bad. She remembered Charlie telling Jon that they were together and Jon's phone calls. She remembered the tears, the words and the anger. But like most things it blew over and if it was not forgotten, it was most definitely forgiven.

Secondly, there was Stripey. A good for nothing Sutton lout, she smirked as she thought back on her nights out with this guy. He was a real piece of work and not worth even thinking about now. He had his uses at the time she thought, but quickly put her mind back to where she was in this beautiful and exotic land, with a man who loved her and she loved back.

She lay down on the bed and hugged her sleeping man, hoping that the future would hold as much as the present did for her.

A couple of hours passed and when Charlie awoke from his deep sleep, he saw Jo at the mirror putting on makeup and doing her hair. She smiled a big beaming grin when he opened his eyes.

"Hello you, I thought you would never wake up – you have been asleep for hours and hours!"

Charlie felt like a great weight had been lifted as he awoke and he was excited about where he was. He had that electric feeling of being somewhere new and unknown and he couldn't wait to explore it.

"What time is it?"

"It is...8.30 in the evening my sweet. You have slept all day. And now it is time to go out!"

"Ok...where are you taking me?"

"Well...wherever you want. But we'll start at some places I know on Khaosan Road."

"Cool."

With that Charlie whipped off the duvet and got ready for a night on the town.

Khaosan Road was a bizarre and quite remarkable spectacle to a new visitor. Full of colour, vigour and life, Charlie was immediately struck by Bangkok and its people. As he opened the double doors of the D and D inn, out into the warm night air, he was greeted with the sounds of street sellers and tourists flocking in the nearby roads.

To his left, he caught the eye of a Thai man standing outside a suit shop. Within an instant the man had ascertained Charlie's nationality and started in on him,

"Geezer! How you doing mate! You like suit, you like Armani, Versace..."

Before Charlie had the time to even look in the window, Jo dragged him away warning him about the persistence of the salesmen. Charlie followed her lead, feeling for the warmth of her hand as her beautiful body shuffled through the crowds and towards the nearest bar.

The first place they stopped at was called The Silk bar. It had an automatic appeal to Charlie as you walked into the bar through a large outside terrace on two levels. There was waitress service, customary in this part of the world and premiership football projected proudly onto one of the outside walls.

As soon as they sat down the waitress came over and taken their order. They were flush as it was the first night, so they ordered beers, cocktails and a plate of Calamari. The bar was busy and multicultural. The bulk of the clientele were from the western world but it was a cosmopolitan place with many people from around the globe.

Charlie and Jo talked excitedly about the trip and what they planned to do. They discussed tentatively about staying in Bangkok for a few days before dropping down to Krabi and the islands of Kho Phi Phi and Kho Phangyan, before taking in a full moon party. After that they should have just enough time to recover before returning home. In all, they had about a month and planned to take things in a relaxed and fancy free manner.

They drank well and when they were inebriated enough they had the bravery to try the local beverage of choice; Sangsom whiskey and Thai Red bull. These drinks were served by the bucket, rather than the glass, leading to some rather interesting nights out for the average tourist. Charlie began to understand, why tourists and travellers spoke so fondly about their trips to this part of the world. It was cheap, exciting and friendly. There was also a sense of *real* freedom, like you could do anything you wanted to do. Charlie was not sure whether this was the country or the bucket in front of him that was causing him to think like this, but either way, he liked it.

After a couple of these devilish concoctions, the world around him became even more blurry and interesting. Jo was under the impression that the Thai version of Red Bull contained speed and as Charlie came to think of it, it wouldn't surprise him.

He paid the bill and they stumbled up Khaosan road to the nearest massage parlour. They paid 300 baht for a herbal massage each. This was about 6 quid in England, so Charlie's feeling of contentment continued as he lay down in his boxer shorts for his rub down.

The massage parlour, like a lot of places in Bangkok, had a really seedy feel to it. They were led into a dark room where there were about four or five double mattresses on the floor. Around the mattresses hung see-through veils; a vain attempt to hide people's privacy. Jo briefly felt bad about the exploitation of people in these types of industries in Asia, but as the soft hands moved powerfully over her lower back, she managed to forget all about her issues and drifted off into a light and pleasant dream.

14

From Bangkok, the couple travelled down to the island of Phangyan and a much more relaxed experience, or so they thought. The time on the island couldn't have started more sweetly, as after a long and tiresome coach and boat journey in the thickness of the Thai heat; they managed to get a free ride to their resort in the back of a jeep. Charlie in a vest with his sunglasses on felt like a king, as the sun heated his skin and the palm trees raced by.

The Green Papaya Resort was something of a luxury by Thai standards. It was set on the beach, in a beautiful cove surrounded by the greenery and lush vegetation the island had to offer. This would normally spark worry into the minds of the travellers; however Jo had been assured that the resort staff spray the area twice daily to eradicate a majority of the 'little beasties' that lurked in the undergrowth. In fact Jo was very pleased with herself, as at one point it looked like they would not find any accommodation on Phangyan at all. She had searched tirelessly with a local travel agent in Bangkok to find somewhere, but with the full moon party looming and it being peak season, their search appeared fruitless. Only a lucky phone call, to an old friend of the Thai agent, secured their booking in what was an idyllic setting. Jo had been to the beach on her last visit, but not been able to afford this particular hotel, so she knew it would impress Charlie which made her glad.

It was a remarkably beautiful place matched with sublime hospitality. The wooden styling of the villas and the greenery and local flowers mixed together in what appeared to the naked eye as a thoroughly natural setting. There was a swimming pool in the centre of the resort which turned into a waterfall at one end. When you were in the pool, at eye level, it gave the impression of a watery oasis, which merged into the sea and the horizon equally. As time passed, Charlie would spend a lot of time on his lilo (he had named Larry), in awe of this visual image, where, it seemed, if he made one wrong turn he could end up falling off the earth into a blissful nirvana of sun and sea.

Charlie had obviously been on numerous beach holidays before, but had never had the freedom he felt he had here. He was usually on quite a strict regime, devised by some of his draconian ex-girlfriends and was never allowed to fulfil a lot of his holiday wishes. He understood, that drunken threesomes would probably be out of the question with Jo, although he did enquire, but to no avail. However, he did always want to hire a motorbike while on his travels and having no license or experience had always been a problem for him in the past. He asked Jo what she thought about it and she agreed, obviously if care was taken and he got used to riding it before taking her on it. Fair play thought Charlie and went straight to hire one from the hotel next door. After all, how hard could it be? 16 year olds in South Croydon were driving these bikes around with no problem every evening after school! Charlie was like a pig in shit, especially since he had a few beers over lunchtime and mixed with the extreme heat and getting his own way, he felt mildly euphoric.

He jumped on the bike and started practising up and down the bumpy road that led into their village.

"Look, it's pretty simple!" He shouted over to Jo as he sputtered up the road, with little control over anything he was doing.

"Well done darling, keep practising. Try and turn honey as well…"

Jo shouted up to him as he continued up the road.

This thought of turning, hadn't really occurred to Charlie and began to fluster him. He decided to turn the handlebars slightly and, with that, his balance and posture were completely lost. He was a large-framed man and at 35 kilometres an hour he, with all his experience, was now in a lot of trouble. He steered the other way to try and correct it, but this only meant he lost even more of his balance. His arse was shifting all over the place on the seat and he was really beginning to panic. Jo was shouting up to him, "Press the brake! The brake Charlie!"

Yet it was to no avail as, in Charlie's panic at hitting the brakes, he didn't realise he was pulling down hard on the throttle. Thus he sped up and sped up until he decided it best (that's what he liked to tell people, really he didn't have a clue what he was doing) to veer off into the plants and long grass at the side of the road.

He fell off the bike and felt largely unscathed, except he could feel the pressure of the bike weighing heavily down on his left calf. Smoke was rising from the machine or his leg and as Jo came running up to him, not knowing whether to laugh or cry, he managed to get the contraption off * him.

"You idiot, Charlie. I told you to take care, are you all right!?"

Charlie mustered a little giggle at the irony of the situation and pulled himself to his feet. Christ knows what he was lying in.

"Yeah, I'm fine. I think I have mastered the bike as well…"

After the debacle with Jen and her boyfriend, things returned largely to normal in our house in Canterbury. My relationship with Brad got back to what it was and in some respects we both grew up a little bit more and put a bit more effort into our studies. As time passed by, I was spending more and more time in the library, with a lot of our pals 'studying' when essentially it was a glorified social club. Brad even popped down a few times, but I am not sure the ambience really suited him. Come to think of it, it didn't really suit any of us.

Anyway, our finals were coming up and I stood myself in a reasonable position to get a 2:1 in English. This was remarkably surprising to me given that, without exaggeration, I had honestly missed around 70% of my lectures. I had no problem downloading the notes and occasionally reading around a subject, but actual lecture and seminar time were a real problem for me. It was never brought up by anyone at the uni. I guess a majority of students here had similar attendances and as long as the money kept rolling in they didn't care. However, I was on about 58% for year 2 and needed to get to 60% overall to get the 2:1. I didn't really have a master plan as to how I was going to do this and given the amount of work I had done, I thought it might be fairer if I got a 2:2.

Brad on the other hand was in a bit of a pickle and needed to pull his finger out if he was to get a degree at all. So he was spending more time than he would normally spend looking over notes and pretending to study. All in all, we had a few months left before the exams and after that the summer ball and a few months of drinking and fun before the real world started for us all.

It turned out that the motorbike, which had been resting on

Charlie's leg, had in fact burned into him and caused him quite a lot of pain. Jo had washed it and wrapped it up for a couple of days but was generally of the opinion it should be left out to heal. Charlie agreed, but the dust, dirt and heat had turned the rather, deep and large wound septic. Over time, the scar which was over three inches long and about two inches wide, became covered in a green and yellow layer that was itchy and painful at the same time. Charlie had a fairly in-depth chat with an Englishman who had bought the local 'reggae' bar in the village. It was a chilled out place which was weed friendly and over a couple of beers and spliffs, the owner brought up the subject of Charlie's leg. He said he had noticed it and thought Charlie should definitely get it looked at in the local hospital, fifteen miles away.

The news from the hospital was not good and after an excruciatingly painful cleaning of the wound, Charlie learned he had to have a drip in his hand and come back to the hospital three times a day for his liquid antibiotics. Not only was this a major headache it also scuppered their plans to move on to Phi Phi after the full moon party. I guess, Charlie thought, it served him right and unfortunately meant there may have been some truth in his nagging girlfriend's thoughts with regards to the dangers of motorbikes. Charlie felt dejected but decided to go to the hotel bar to order some calamari and a Long Island iced tea. As he sat down and watched the sun melt into the sea on the horizon, his mood suddenly lifted.

One of the main attractions of a holiday in Thailand is the full moon party at Haad Rin, Kho Phangyan and since a majority of the nights spent together on this island had been relatively tame by Charlie's standards, he was keen to make sure they made the most of it.

Jo was keen also to see a bit of the island and decided they would take a trip on the bike (Charlie had become a little more skilled on it over time), one evening. It was the night before the full moon party so Jo had thought that Haad Rin, would be fairly quiet in the build up to tomorrow night. The sun was shining and the sky was clear so they set out on the bike to find their bearings and to get a bite to eat and a drink on the other side of the island.

The roads, as always, were clear and Charlie and Jo chatted quite happily as they made their way along the bumpy tracks. Charlie fancied himself as a modern day Steve Macqueen, now he had mastered the art of riding this contraption and his scar was healing nicely.

As night fell, though, they found themselves a good 15km from Haad Rin. The roads were getting muddier, narrower and hillier though and the heavens felt like they were about to open as the heavens were inclined to do at this time of year, in this climate. The pair were just in shorts and t-shirts and needless to say the rain came down in buckets causing the two to come off the road and stop in at a local Thai bar, of the ropiest variety. After a couple of beers, they decided to continue the journey as the rain seemed ceaseless and time was marching on.

The hills however were getting steeper and steeper to the point where it was becoming a serious worry to the couple on their 100cc splutterer. Not to mention, Charlie and Jo, were not the slightest of people and momentum was being lost in the hills at an alarming rate. On top of this, the traffic was building up in preparation for the big night the next day. The situation came to a head when Charlie came upon what he believed, in no uncertain terms, to be a mountain on the way to Haad Rin. He was literally at a right angle, with Jo screaming at him, clinging onto his t-shirt for dear life. Charlie pulled the throttle right back and leaned his body forward but, alas, this was to no avail, as the bike under their weight, gave up the ghost and started moving backwards. Charlie would not have minded so much but there was a drink delivery truck ploughing up the hill in the darkness, honking his horn with fervour, getting closer and closer. The two dragged the bike to the side of the road and hid from the oncoming traffic in the brush and hedges.

By this stage Charlie was severely irritated and had lashed out at Jo who was equally rattled. She stormed off in the pouring rain, while Charlie watched her; he struggled soaking from sweat and rain with the bike he felt like letting go of, off the side of the cliff. Charlie thought this would be a wonderful metaphor for something or other, maybe for a music video, where a man truly hits rock bottom after losing everything.

Somehow, Charlie and Jo made it to Haad Rin in one piece. The rain clouds had eased off and as the heat rose in the thick night, they found that a majority of their clothes had dried and equally spirits were much higher than they had been about half an hour before. There were still quite a few drinkers and revellers around, despite the party the following day, as they drove into Haad Rin town centre and parked up.

First stop was a bar to have a couple of beers, before heading onto a pretty little pizzeria near the main strip and the beach. The food was good, if a little expensive by Thai standards, but filled the hole and provided enough wine for Jo to forget her inhibitions, like her wet shorts and bikini bottoms, and how they intended to get home that evening.

The conversation flowed freely and it didn't take long before they both had that warm gooey feeling of happiness and tipsiness that they had become so accustomed to.

"After this, if we pop down to the beach I will show you a few places you might like. There are some good bars and magic mountain."

"Magic Mountain? Where are we, in a Disney film?" mused Charlie.

"Ha ha, no you will see what I mean when you finish your drink slow coach!" Jo retorted. With that, Charlie finished up his glass of wine, paid the bill and followed her out of the restaurant.

They walked down the quaint little street and onto the beach where again Charlie found himself impressed by the view of the bay area in front of him. On the horizon there were lights from a distant ship and he could make out the mountainous edges of the bay and some rocks leading out to sea. As he looked from the edge inland slightly, he saw the famed Magic Mountain mentioned previously. It stood high above the rest of the town and was connected to the beach by a series of wooden steps. Charlie could make out a bright neon sign with the bar's name on and it seemed like it was pretty full with people. There was the distant bass of chilled out house music and Charlie found himself drawn to the place.

"So there it is babe, fancy going up there?" asked Jo.

Charlie could hazard a guess as to what the bar sold, but he thought he would ask anyway. He liked to give Jo the satisfaction of knowing something he didn't. Plus, it didn't happen very often so he asked it.

"What is it, just a bar?"

"No babe, it is a magic mushroom place, but you can get beers as well," replied Jo.

"Cool, I am up for it. Have you done them before? Mushrooms?" asked Charlie tentatively.

"Yeah I have done them. It didn't do much to me though; I think I was more drunk than anything last time." She replied flippantly.

Charlie was always a bit wary of people who claimed drugs did nothing to them. He put this down to Jo not wanting to lose face or sound uncool, bless her. She knew that Charlie had taken a lot more drugs than her and probably didn't want to feel out of place, or as if she was not streetwise. Charlie had mates in the past that had taken drugs like heroin and claimed that it had done nothing to them or just given them a stomach ache or something like that. All Charlie knew is that whenever he had taken mushrooms, or in fact any drug really, it had had an effect. That's why he liked them. Charlie just smiled at his fiancée and linked hands as they moved up towards Magic Mountain.

The final exams went smoothly and I felt I had done reasonably well. I was not fussed about what degree level I came out with as I had such an interesting time in Canterbury, the level of degree didn't really affect me. What was more pleasing was that Brad felt his exams went well and he would get out of there with a pass or a third.

Anyway, all eyes were on the summer ball now and despite the furore of our final year and my infidelity, Bobby had remained loyal to me and was coming down for it. We had been separated for quite a while due to the final examinations and the way the timings had fallen over the past couple of months. Although, I was not massively ambitious, she was and hoped to achieve a first in Mathematics at Leeds University. She was in with a shot, so worked incredibly hard in the run up to the exams and essentially hid herself away for the past few months.

Bobby was up for it now though and had come to Canterbury for a few days, which incorporated the summer ball. I was excited, although a little nervous about the people Bobby may run into at the ball. There were a few skeletons from my years at university I didn't particularly want Bobby to find out about, and the potential was there for a few surprises.

The night however was one I will never forget. Suits were bought, drugs were taken and champagne was drunk over the course of what was an unforgettable evening. I saw all of my friends and we hugged, kissed and danced in what was an orgy of goodwill and joy, laced with cocaine and champagne; the icing on a bitter sweet cake that lasted three years which I will never forget.

15

Charlie and Jo made their way up the crooked steps of Magic Mountain which were relatively treacherous and covered in algae from the sea and the beach. They dropped their shoes at the door which was customary for an establishment such as this and made their way to the bar.

It was 500 baht for a mushroom cocktail and Charlie thought that it would be a good way to start the proceedings and party for tomorrow night. Jo was also in accordance and thought they might start off with one and see how things went. It was essentially foul and was difficult to drink so it was pleasing that they could share it slowly. Charlie also decided to go to the bar and order a beer to wash the taste away. He sat down and felt a relaxation fall over his shoulders and arms, he was chatting to Jo but drifting in and out of remembering what he was saying and just drivelling on in a daze. As Jo didn't seem to care, neither did he and so they just carried on chatting, watching the sea and drifting in and out of consciousness.

That was of course until Charlie noticed something worryingly creep into the corner of his eye line. Had common sense prevailed, he would have known that what he was witnessing could only be a figment of his imagination but instead, panic and paranoia swept through his stomach and he began to sweat. What he saw, was an old cow skull hovering in the sky. It was wearing a dark moleskin cowboy hat and had two red dots for eyes, which kept pulsating bigger then smaller and so on. Now, a cow skull is quite a sinister image at the best of times but in his paranoid state, Charlie became increasingly perturbed.

"What's up honey? You seem stressed?" Jo asked kindly.

"Look! Look it's staring at me!" He hissed.

"Who is staring at you?"

"The cow skull. Look, it's looking at me, it's getting angry!?"

"Charlie, what!?" The perspiration dripped off his face and onto his clothes. Jo couldn't really contain herself much longer, before bursting out into a chuckle, at her poor deluded fiancé. At this point, Charlie finished his beer and went to find his shoes to get himself away from the mad, laughing cow skull.

Needless to say, the ball lasted well into the morning. There were house parties at many old friends' houses where weed and booze and good stories were shared. The sun came up and the parties continued. Bobby went back to the house to sleep, while the boys and I stayed out to chat and reminisce some more. I was becoming more and more pleased with Bobby, it was not so long ago she would have ordered me to return with her, but she was becoming more accommodating as time went on. We were also getting to the point where we had to decide what we were going to do when uni was over. Should we move back home with our parents to save some money or take the big plunge and move in together? Either way I didn't want to think about it now. At this point in time I just wanted to stay with these pals. It was such a shame that the good times never lasted for ever. They were only really brief moments of time we clung too. One thing I did learn though and Bobby would come to learn, is that holding onto something too tight, meant you had already lost it.

Charlie was seriously wasted. But like with all the times he had done mushrooms, they were playing little tricks on his brain and this time was no different. He would spend about half an hour feeling completely out of it, sweaty and paranoid and as high as a kite, whilst the next half hour he would feel completely sober and ready for anything. This was a pattern he was used to with mushrooms and to be honest, that was the fun part of it. One minute, he would be advocating he drove them home over the hills and dirt roads of Phangyan. The next, he would have fallen over in fits and giggles, crying with laughter. What was more disturbing to him though, was that Jo seemed largely unfazed by the mushroom drink at all. I'm such a lightweight giggled Charlie to himself.

They made an executive decision to not to drive back given Charlie's history on the bike and tried to find a taxi that would take them. Eventually they managed to convince a local guy with a 10-seater open back taxi to take them and the bike back. He strapped the bike with a bit of cloth he had found, onto one of the tow bars on the vehicle. He told us to sit in the cab and hold the bike when we went up and down the steep hills, make sure it didn't fall out. Charlie was far more concerned about either of them falling out the back, given their state! The farcical nature of the situation seemed to make Charlie sober up a bit and he took ultimate responsibility for the well being of the bike as they powered their way home. Jo seemed to relax as Charlie gained some sort of composure and as she let the wind blow through her hair in the dark night and the leaves whistle in the wind, she started giggling to the point where she couldn't stop.

"What is it Jo, are you ok?" Charlie said, sniggering at her himself. By this stage, she was in absolute fits of hysterical laughter and pointing outside.

"What is it? What's up!?" Charlie asked again.

Jo was smiling so hard she couldn't speak. She tried to pull her cheeks down so she could get the words out of her mouth, but to no avail. So, she kept pointing outside to the jungle, flanking the roads they were driving down.

"It's…out there…what's doing it…out there..!" she finally spurted out.

Charlie looked out at the blank darkness and the moon and the stars and burst out laughing. They didn't stop until well inside their villa, with the bike safely stowed away by the Thai cab driver. Charlie never remembered how much money he gave the guy, only that he was very grateful as they stumbled and snorted back to the safety of their bedroom.

Brad, Harry, Josh and I eventually finished partying about 10.30am and decided to make our way back home. There was talk of us going all the way through, and doing it again but it had been a long and heavy day of drinking, followed by a heavy night and a bit of morning. It was tempting, but common sense prevailed and we went home to bed. Bobby was crashed out in the front room* when I got there, so I took her up to my room. We made love very lazily, which was still pretty satisfying for both of us, since she was half asleep and I was half cut it felt nice. Her body was warm from sleeping and her breath felt hot on my skin as I moved inside her and caressed her smoothness. It didn't take long and she didn't seem to care, whispering 'I love you' in my ear as we turned away from each other and crashed out.

We slept soundly until about 7pm and the alarm went off on Bobby's phone. I forgot she had work and was getting the train back home to south east London. She had left Leeds behind having been sick of the lifestyle and the people she lived with. So she was going back early to London. She had contacted her old manager at Goldsmiths on Bluewater and taken her old job back. Like most women, she didn't enjoy sitting around and 'wasting time' as she put it. She would rather be 'out there' making money and doing something productive.

I got up and changed and kissed her goodbye and promised I would be back in London in a couple of days. She seemed in good spirits as we parted and I for one felt quite positive about our relationship. I only hoped that would last.

16

The full moon party was really quite a spectacle. There were people from all over the world dressed up, covered in body paint and partying hard. The streets were filled with drinkers and revellers and when you got to the beach, it was hard to find a bit of space because it was all taken up by snake charmers, fire eaters and so on. As much as it was a good laugh, Charlie and Jo were not 100% up for it due to the night before. They toyed with the idea of going to Magic Mountain, but thought about the queues and the distance and decided to give it a miss. Needless to say they drank themselves into a state with Sangsom and Red Bull and made a real go of the evening. They danced on the beach, chatted to other travellers and watched the moon as it softly sprinkled its light onto the peaceful sea.

Tiredness set in not long after midnight and after a bite to eat they decided to make the journey back to their resort and turn in. They both found it heart-warming mind you that there were places in the world where people do still come together and enjoy life to the fullest. The news was full of depressing stories back home of gang violence, knife crime and murder. But here it seemed as if everyone had a common goal, which was fuelled by love and that was a great feeling.

Josh had got up from his slumber and was watching TV downstairs in a white t-shirt and boxer shorts. He was one of our housemates and one of my good friends. He was a popular guy around campus and had various different friendship groups around town. He was in the football team and therefore was not often around the house and has not yet been introduced into this story.

"Hello mate," I said with a cheeky smile on my face.

"Bonjour!" This was one of his customary phrases. "Has Bobby gone?"

"Yes, she has to work tomorrow so she is going back to London." I replied.

"Sweet!" Josh beamed at me.

"Why's that mate?"

"Well, I think we should go out tonight, for old time's sake and that!" He replied.

"Seriously? After the ball and all the money and…" I pleaded.

"Fuck that, let's go we are not going to be here much longer, get your gear on."

I could never really say no if something was offered to me, but even more so if Josh offered it. He had one of those infectious characters. He oozed charisma and more importantly, he would pretty much always guarantee you a good night out. So, I decided to resist arguing with him and saved my energy. I thought I would probably be needing it.

I went and spruced up, had a shower and popped some half clean clothes on. Given the ball was just last night, I looked ok. The bags under my eyes were there, but overall I hadn't scrubbed up too badly. I went into Brad's room and Josh was in there puffing on a rather large skunk bong.

"Jeez…" I said, a little concerned about the state we were going to get ourselves in. I was still pissed and had the shakes from the night before.

Brad passed me over the bong.

"Go on son, you know it makes sense…" he slurred.

Like I said, I could never refuse a kind gesture so took a big puff and got ready to leave the house.

The plane touched down and even before the doors had opened, you could tell you were back in England. Charlie always got a numb feeling about returning home. There was a slight pleasure somewhere inside of him to be back and return to normality but there was such a grey despondence about his homeland he always felt a bit annoyed about. It was always raining or cloudy upon arrival. It was often very cold too. He looked around and saw the grey buildings of West London, the tarmac, the car parks. It was hardly the thick warmth and colour of Asia, but at least he was home and even though he was not that happy to be home, he did have a new excitement about helping out with the wedding. Not to mention he was looking forward to seeing his Father *who according to reports had responded well to his treatment.

Charlie and Jo had about a week before school started again and they planned to relax and see some friends before that. There were to visit Charlie's father in a couple of days and also get a 'wedding update' from Jo's parents and see what was needed to be done. They had less than a year now, which was a concern to Jo, even though it seemed like an eternity to Charlie.

We made our way across to the Tenet to see who was about and what the vibe was like. The town seemed quiet, however it was a Thursday night and it was possible that some hardcore students would be around, or at least some from Kent and also some town folk might be out for a pre-weekend drink up.

The Tenet was fairly busy. It was not like it usually was at 9.15pm on a Thursday, but there were some faces from our college around that we knew. I was feeling pretty ill from the lager last night and although the bong had taken the edge off of my hangover, the thought of another beer was not filling me with joy. So I started on the gin and tonics, nice and quaffable, I thought. What I did find though was they were going down a bit too quickly and I was finishing way ahead of Brad and Josh. So I moved onto pints of Strongbow. I was feeling pretty wasted and could hear myself slurring when I talked which is never a good sign. If you are beginning to think you are on your way to being pissed, you most often already are. I took solace in the fact though, that my mates must be about as pissed as me, thank god.

"So, things all right with Bobby? She seemed to have a good time last night?" asked Brad, while Josh was chatting to some of his pals from the football team.

"Yeah. I am feeling pretty good about it all really. She was much more chilled and passive than she has been before when we have gone out, so…"

"Well, it was your ball, man. She wouldn't want to fuck that up. She would never have been forgiven!" Brad replied.

"True. I think she is making more of an effort though in general to be more…I don't know…"

"Amenable?" Brad said.

"Yeah, I guess so, more willing to let me do what I want, maybe…" I said a little bit proud of how she was willing to change. I always knew she loved me, but she was never really willing to compromise. It was always her way of the highway in the past.

"Uh-huh. But why do you think that is? Do you think she has just changed, or does she want something?" Brad asked.

I knew my mates were trying to look out for me but they always seemed to have it in for Bobby, no matter what. They couldn't be happy that she had been better; there was always an ulterior motive in their eyes.

"Look, what's the problem? She was cool. Maybe she is growing up. Maybe she is changing, I don't know! Maybe, she wants me to move in with her or something when we get home." I replied getting a little frayed around the edges.

"Exactly mate. I don't want to piss on your cornflakes or anything, but women don't just change out of nowhere from my experience. She clearly wants something. Sorry, but I just don't want you to get played by any woman, not just Bobby." Brad replied softly.

I had noticed Josh had come back over and although he wasn't saying anything, I could tell he agreed with Brad. He looked at me and then looked away. With that the seed of doubt was planted.

"Played? By her? I think not mate. Are we going to go on from here then, later on?" I asked.

"Where do you want to go?" Josh asked with a mischievous smile across his face.

17

Time flew by fairly quickly as the couple got back to work and back into a regular routine. A lot of weekends were taken up by doing things for the wedding like tasting food and wine, trying out various hotels and visiting local churches. Jo was largely an atheist but Charlie was brought up a Catholic. He took his first communion but bowed out of being confirmed for a variety of reasons. Charlie was a bright young boy who took an interest in religious studies at school. He was open to new ideas and beliefs and so on and found a lot of Catholic teachings outdated and irrelevant. He also found a lot of them very useful too, but for him the negative teachings about sex and love outweighed the good. He didn't believe that homosexuals were wrong, or that condoms were the work of the devil. At his tender age and the grammar school girls he went around with, without condoms, he would have no chance of getting any action whatsoever! He was also a bit aggravated about the teachings on divorce and abortion. His mother had been through both and god knows the guilt and anguish she suffered due to the attitudes of the church, when really the only person to blame for both was Charlie's father.

In all honesty a lot of his problem lay in the fact that his Mother insisted on taking him to the Sunday morning mass at 8.30am. It was good because it was slightly quicker than the main mass at 10.30am, but Charlie was beginning to discover drinking and girls at the age of 13 and quite often he was not in a fit state to be going anywhere at this hour on a Sunday morning. So he packed it in, much to the disgruntlement of his mother.

Catholicism however, had got to him at an early age and therefore he was still touched by the faith and although confused like a lot of Catholics. He wanted to honour his mother's beliefs and in some respects his own. To that end, Jo had agreed to have a church wedding although she drew the line at a Catholic service and the rigmorale one had to go through to have one.

Charlie was beginning again to find this part of the wedding a little bit tiresome and began to feel bogged down. He needed something a little bit selfish and for himself and after a brief chat with his closest friends, he made the decision to have his stag 'do' in Las Vegas. This was going to be expensive but Charlie had good friends and was certain ten of his friends would be up for the trip. In reality, only seven made it, largely due to some spinelessness of one, the pecuniary problems of another and the ongoing health issues of his father. Either way, a trusty seven were booked and ,all in all, it was a good crowd. Charlie and company looked forward to the trip greatly.

They were to travel at Easter as the weather would be good but not too hot and also was a safe enough distance from the wedding to not cause any major issue. So they only had a few months to save money and so the months following Christmas remained relatively quiet.

"I am definitely getting some pussy tonight!" Josh announced to us, as we finished our pints at a rapid pace.

We had a few more drinks and then a shot of sambuca as we left the pub and jumped in a taxi up to Kent University. We felt that it would be livelier up there as they had their ball next week, so more people would be around. I was in a real state and decided it would be best to put my phone on silent because, if Bobby called, I would get serious earache for going out again. We were talking loudly in the car and the other two seemed pretty wasted too, which made me feel a little better. Despite our respective states, we were let into The Venue with relative ease and we could see why, as it was pretty quiet. It was, on the whole, about a third full but there were still enough people to give it an atmosphere and to disguise our loud drunkenness.

Josh walked across the dance floor and introduced himself to almost every girl who was half-decent looking, slurring 'evening treacle' and 'would you like a drink sweet cheeks?' with that big, confident grin across his face. He very rarely got any attitude from girls, despite his upfront manner. God knows, Brad and I would be slapped almost every time if we tried it, but Josh just had a way with people; especially women.

Another one of his tricks would be to go up behind a girl and tap her on the shoulder or slap her arse and when she turned around point at me or Brad and start telling us off. He almost always got away with that too. There was a lot to be said for that sort of charm and I knew that all too well.

I was so wasted, that I was beginning to share Josh's lust this evening. I was watching even moderately attractive girls on the dance floor and thinking all sorts of dirty thoughts. Before the evening began, I really wanted to try and do the right thing by Bobby. But it was virtually impossible with the mates I had around me. They got me to thinking again about how manipulative she was and as the drinks went down I began to think that she must have cheated on me too. She had been at Leeds for three years, not to mention the fact that her ex-boyfriend lived a few roads down from her. I convinced myself that she must be some cheap slut, taking it every which way and so I was going to make sure, I was not the one left on my own, looking like a mug.

"Joshsshh…let's pull one of thesssee gahhlllss…" I slurred, whilst spilling my vodka diet coke all over my jeans.

"Well, we could do but you can hardly stand up! Who do you reckon then?"

"…don't care mate, whoever is easiest…." I replied.

"Fair enough! Give me ten minutes." Josh replied full of confidence and chuckling to himself.

I leaned myself up against a pillar in the club and tried to look vaguely sober. Brad just looked at me and bellowed with laughter.

I was sitting in the cab with Josh and two girls who went to Kent University. We were chatting away, god knows about what, with Josh largely leading the conversation and saying all the right things. I had established we were going back to their house which was not too far away on the West side of the city and I was trying my level best to remain in the game and not to look too foolish.

I can only imagine what Josh had said to this poor girl to get her to take me home. It really is a mystery. She had a 6 foot 2 inch bloke she had never met before, stumbling up to her doorstep, making no coherent sense. It was doubtful I would get it up and even if I did this performance was going to be shit without doubt. We parted company from Josh and his girl as they decided on a few more drinks in the front room when they arrived home. My one had decided that may not be such a good idea and we headed straight up to her room.

I needed to get it together a little bit, so headed for the bathroom and went to the toilet, slapping water in my face. I looked peaky but composed myself and went back to her room. I always got a little nervous in this situation and never wanted to be presumptuous about what was going to happen, so I made a bit of small talk with her. I found out she was from Erith in South London (which helped explain how I got the invite home so easily. Girls from around those parts did carry with them quite a reputation) and she was in her second year. I decided to keep facts about me to a minimum as Christ knows what yarn Josh had spun to get me there. Maybe I was studying law or was an aspiring singer; I wouldn't have put it past him to come up with some rubbish like that. Anyway, I didn't have to hold my own too long because the minute she went to the bathroom, I was out like a light fully clothed on this stranger's bed.

7

Charlie had been to Las Vegas once before when he was 16 years old with his father. Firstly, in 1997, Las Vegas was a bit different. Yes it was still vast and unbelievable but it was like window shopping when you are that age. You can look but not touch, since laws to do with gambling and drinking were so stringent in the U.S.

My father used to let me share his vodka and have a few beers in his hotel room but as for drinking in the casinos, not a chance.

Furthermore, this was the first time I had flown into Vegas and it was quite something. The airport is so close to the strip, at one stage during landing, I was sure the pilot had miscalculated and was going to set her down right by Caesar's Palace!

I felt like I was a kid again, in shock and awe at the magnitude of the place. So much time and effort was put into making everything perfect for the tourists. It was remarkable.

We got into the bar of the Treasure Island complex, where we were staying and got straight onto the beers, ready to plan our first night here. Conversely, we made the executive decision not to plan anything this trip and see where it would take us. As night began to fall, we decided to get our Glad rags on and meet back in the bar in half an hour to really 'attack the night', as my best man Steve, so deftly put it.

I woke up first and god knows what time it was. We were both naked and I was seriously worried about how I smelt after the last couple of days. I rolled out of bed, put on this girl's dressing gown and went to the bathroom for a brief wash. I looked like shit and was undoubtedly still drunk but didn't feel that bad yet. I looked at my cock and decided that we hadn't had sex last night. After washing it, I could tell for sure we hadn't as there was no smell of rubber and definitely no smell of anything else. Poor girl, I thought. I had better make it up to her now. I got back in the room and she was stirring.

"How are you? You want a cup of tea?" She asked politely.

"No, thanks. I am fine. How are you? Can't remember much of what happened last night." I asked tentatively.

She chuckled, "Don't worry; you were no danger to anyone last night. You crashed out in all your clothes!" She said.

She didn't seem too annoyed, which was pleasing. I had got back into bed and moved in closer to her, holding her body from behind. She moved her leg in-between mine and placed my hand on the curve of her arse. She was a petite young girl and the way she was so chilled about last night really started to turn me on. If this was Bobby, I would be getting all sorts of grief about getting too drunk and being a disappointment. That did remind me, where was my phone? I looked around and saw my jeans at the bottom of the bed. I must have kicked them off in my sleep. Oh well, I will worry about that later, I thought.

"So the earth didn't really move for you last night then?" I asked her with a smile.

"The earth? I am not even sure the bed moved once!" She laughed and turned her body to face me. She was pretty, without being stunning and had mousey brown hair. She was quintessentially English in lots of ways. None more so however, than when she put her hand on my cock and started kissing my neck.

"You can always make up for it now…" she trailed off and kissed my chest and stomach before taking my cock in her mouth.

I was so horny, from the drink and drugs I decided it was best to come in her mouth, as again performance would be nothing short of lacklustre the first time around. She purred as I came and looked straight in my eyes as she swallowed and I fell very briefly in love or at least what felt like love. I was developing a soft spot for this girl, even though I didn't even know her name. I flipped her over firmly but softly enough to be playful and began kissing her neck and her breasts. I went down on her until she came and the sounds of her little whimpers and moans had got me aroused to hardness again. We had sex in four or five different positions and it felt as if we really connected as a couple. She worked hard in bed, unlike a lot of females I had relations with and really wanted to please.

After it was over, I didn't really want to leave or in fact lose contact with her. So I hung around and had a cup of tea, her mate from last night was there but Josh was long gone. My phone had died which provided a pleasant refuge from Bobby for a brief moment in time.

I finished my drink and decided to get out of her hair. I discovered the girl's name was Emma when I asked her to put her number in my phone. We kissed goodbye and I left, knowing that I would probably never see her or speak to her again. I felt though if only for a night, I had fallen in love as I was prone to doing. I tried to blank out the little pangs of guilt and hurt and concentrate on the stories I had to tell the boys when I arrived back home. It was sad that was what it all boiled down to in the end, a cheap laugh for my mates.

I wished she could know how she had made me feel. I wanted to tell her that this meant something, but knew in reality I couldn't. I hated the thought that she would spend the day watching 'Friends' boxsets in her room, feeling used and unwanted. I wanted to tell her that the first thing I would do when I got home was text her and organise a meal out or a drink, but I knew I wouldn't. I was a coward. As much as I told myself I would break up with Bobby and try something new, something that made me happy; I knew It would never happen.

Excitement brewed as Charlie and his friends downed beers quickly at the Breeze bar in Treasure Island. They were being waited on by a scantily-clad cocktail waitress and she was giving them the lowdown on good places to go that evening. The general consensus was that Coyote Ugly in the Paris hotel was an interesting place to head to. But not before the boys met up with some girls Steve knew from back home.

We headed over to see the gondolas and bridges of The Venetian which were quite spectacular really as the canals went through the building and if one was so inclined, you could take a trip for a certain fee.

We did a little bit of gambling with little success and continued to take in the ambience of this mystical city. As the beers flew down, our pace quickened and we moved from casino to casino, popping over to Caesar's Palace and The Bellagio before getting a cab up to 'New York, New York.' The girls who were from Surrey back home had mixed rather nicely with our group and they added a bit of spice to the evening. Las Vegas was not the sort of place where picking up girls was that easy, so this was a welcome surprise for Charlie and his entourage.

They queued up and made their way into Coyote Ugly which was a little disappointing in all honesty. It was quite small and not at all like the film. But there were some fantastic looking people present and so the boys were kept happy by having a dance and trying hard to get chatting to some of the Vegas girls.

Charlie at one point lost his pals, only to find a few of them whispering in the ear of the girl on stage who was the compere for the evening. Automatically this filled him with dread as he was not one for exhibitionism and he could only imagine what they were asking was to do with him.

As the song playing finished, Charlie felt a sense of dread in his stomach as the compere picked up the microphone.

"Ladies and gentlemen, we have a very special person here getting married in a few months time, on their stag do!"

Cunts, thought Charlie.

"Could Charlie please make his way to the stage!" She continued.

The thought of bolting out the door did cross his mind, but the boys had thought of that and a few of them were behind him, clearly on guard duty.

Charlie approached the stage and jumped on and the rest to him was a bit of a blur. He remembered being told repeatedly that he was a 'bad boy' and 'needed to be taught a lesson' and then he remembers a lot of flash photography and being spanked over and over again.

Charlie was seriously embarrassed here as pretty much all the lady folk in the building took their turn bending him over and beating his arse and he felt sweat drip off his face and onto the floor. It was horrible. The only saving grace to proceedings was being given a multitude of shots by the hot Coyote Ugly girl afterwards, which did take the edge off his shame. He returned back to the group to much backslapping and cheering but ultimately he felt horrible so took refuge talking to one of the prettier more sympathetic girls in the group.

He was getting on with her well but thought nothing of it what with him getting married and being on a stag do, he knew that he could talk freely with her knowing there was no undercurrent. No self-respecting girl Charlie knew would want to get with him given the public display of his betrothal the club had just been told about. Thankfully, I am safe and can relax, Charlie thought to himself.

As I arrived at the house all the boys were in. Josh had already started packing his things away to go home and Brad was upstairs jamming on his guitar. It turned out the girl was leading Josh on and so he decided it best to leave to save hassle for both of them. I told him my war stories and thanked him for coming through for me as always. He laughed and cursed his luck at picking the wrong girl!

We spent the rest of the day packing up the kitchen and having a real sort out, I eventually turned my phone back on and had 42 missed calls from Bobby. I rang her back and she was in a terrible state. She was clearly worried about me and called me all the names under the sun. I told her my phone had died when I was out last night and when I woke up this morning, Brad had locked my charger in his room so I had to wait for him to get back from wherever he was to charge it up. I would have called from someone else's phone but no-one was in…

It was a shitty thing to lie about, but what else could I say? I was a cheating bastard, like my father before me and his father too. There is no excuse for it and the guilt the next day always got you back for the good times the night before.

I managed to calm her down and promised her I would be home the next day to see her. Once the house was packed up and sorted, we all convened downstairs for a chat and to watch a bit of TV. That was the way in which university finished for me. The three most intriguing and educational years of my life for a variety of reasons, ended in the words of T.S. Eliot, not with a bang but a whimper.

18

Her name was Debbie and as Charlie was kissing her at the bar, he wondered how on earth he managed to get himself in these situations. He really loved Jo and by hook or by crook he would make it work with her, but here he was about to get it on, with some girl who lived down the road from Jo, back home. Nice one, Charlie thought. He was the only stag that could come to Las Vegas and shit on his own doorstep.

"Listen you are lovely and that, but I am in love with another girl. This doesn't make sense, really," Charlie asked. Hoping this girl would see sense at some stage.

"I know and I don't really care. Surely you want one more night of freedom before you get married? No strings…if you like…" Debbie purred.

She sure managed to put together a strong case as she pulled him by the shirt towards her and kissed him deeply again.

Before Charlie knew it, she was whispering in his ear to take her upstairs and fuck her senseless. Charlie was up for it, but felt bad and peeked over at his friends sitting and talking around a table near the bar. Steve looked over furtively, before Charlie was dragged towards the lifts, towards Debbie's room.

I returned home and after initial feelings of disappointment; I managed to adapt to life back at home. I had moved back in temporarily with my Mum which was not a major issue for me, as I had grown up a lot since I was the young boy who left for college, thinking I was going thousands of miles away with a load of unknown people. I remember crying on that first night at university. I had unpacked all my belongings and put them out just as they were in my room in my Mother's house. I looked around the room whilst listening to my other housemates getting to know each other and sharing a beer on the first night. I stared at my posters and burst into tears. Immediately, I rang my Mum and although she was initially upset to hear me sad, she told me to get out there and start talking to people. I felt in a way she was being cruel, but really it was the best advice. I tidied myself up and went out there and never looked back.

That first night we went to a nearby bar, just for a few drinks as we were all tired and were saving ourselves for the 'fresher's ball' the following night. We ended up getting wasted, buying weed and coming back to the flat. We smoked and laughed and I realised that I could be around other people and survive. I thought before the night was out that I had been happier than ever before and couldn't wait to get my teeth into university life. I thought about the phone call I had made to my Mum and was so grateful to her for pushing me through school and bailing me out financially to get me to university. She was desperate for me to go and her reasons were a million miles from mine for me being there. But, we had met in the middle and both were as happy as could be and this was down to her making something of my life and I can't thank her enough for that.

Anyway, I was back in her house now which although she didn't mind, we both knew I needed to get sorted and get a place of my own. The most viable option was with Bobby. I was still pretty undecided as to what I would do with my life, but through all the bullshit and the pain, I loved Bobby and she did represent a level of solidity I needed.

I went to see my Father and talked to him about what I should do next. I was employed, working at Virgin Megastores in Bluewater. This was fine for the summer, but I needed to do something with more longevity and definitely more pay!

"I don't know Dad, what shall I do? They are talking about promoting me to a senior sales rep at Virgin."

"Oh, what's that? A pay rise to £6 an hour?" He said mockingly, "that's not going to do son, is it?" He retorted.

"Well-what then? It's not like I could do what you do is it?" My father was a teacher and he was good at it. I had seen him a few times and he was a natural. A lot of the kids liked him and if they didn't like him they were scared of him and that was enough to make it work.

"Well, why not? You have got the degree, you just have to do another year and get the certificate. Even if you don't become a teacher, it is always something to fall back on." He said with surprising enthusiasm.

"But you and Mum always moan about teaching! All the time!" I replied.

"Well, it's a hard job son, but the pay is getting better and as long as you don't let the bastards grind you down..." he trailed off.

"Really?" I replied and got lost deep in thought.

"But, I got expelled from school Dad, I was a little shit – no thanks to you!" I smiled at him, thinking about the times he had kept me off to see his friends from overseas and to go to cricket matches.

" Yeah, so was I? Sometimes the little shits make the best teachers." He smiled at me and leant his head to one side, looking me up and down.

With that, the seed was planted. I looked into enrolling on a PGCE course, checked out the pay, thought about the holidays and I was decided. I enlisted on a course at the University of Surrey in Roehampton and rented a flat in a lovely residential area in Wimbledon.

There was only one slight problem with this plan, Bobby's reaction. I had kept her vaguely in the loop about the teaching course, but hadn't told her about the flat in Wimbledon or the fact that I was starting in a couple of weeks, at the end of the summer.

I invited her around for dinner at Mum's to put it to her, over a glass of wine and the safety of my home

"Bobby, you know the teaching thing..?" I started over dinner and Bobby's second glass of rose.

"Yes," she said with a happy tone.

"Well, I have decided to do it, I think." I waited to see what she would say, but she only waited for me to finish.

"Yep, I have enrolled in the English course at Roehampton. It starts in September." I waited for the crash of lightning and thunder to darken the sky, but no such thing occurred.

"Bobby..?" I murmured as she grinned across the table.

"I thought you might, so it's a good thing I signed up for the Maths course at Roehampton too! I start the same day as you! She said. I wanted to surprise you tonight, I knew you would do it!"

"Oh...that's brilliant! No...it's so good, so we can meet for lunch and stuff. Cool!" I tried to sound excited too and from Bobby's reaction I was being relatively convincing.

"No, silly...we can move in together – over there! It makes perfect sense, we can live together!"

She jumped up from the table and gave me a big hug. I felt very mixed up inside. Every avenue I ever had for freedom, she blocked. Maybe this is love, I thought? Maybe we would be happy together? I tried to convince myself, but only felt a dull ache in my heart and a searing resentment pass through my mind.

19

Charlie was outside the door of Debbie's room as she fumbled for her card to open it. He could have been on any floor of any Las Vegas hotel. In fact he could have sworn it was his floor as it was almost identical. Before he could think anymore, he was being tugged into the open doorway and was flung on the bed. Charlie wondered whether Debbie was better looking than Jo. She did seem pretty fit, Debbie, but Charlie had been drinking for hours and hours and knew that she couldn't be as amazing as he thought. One of his first rules was to not go out for a burger when there was steak at home, which was a phrase he stole from one of the actors, Paul Newman or Steve McQueen? Or was it, Frank Sinatra? Anyway, one of his first major rules he appeared on the point of breaking. He was so drunk, he tried to focus on the task in hand and managed to snap Debbie's bra off as she straddled him on her king-size bed.

She gyrated hard on top of him and every time Charlie leaned up to gain control, she pushed him back onto the mattress and kissed him harder. She was a sexy girl Charlie thought and he hardened as she kissed his chest. Suddenly, there was a sharp knock on the door.

"Debbie! Debbie! Can we talk to you? Debbie, it's important," came a stern female voice from outside.

Debbie put her finger on my lips and motioned me to be silent.

"Debbie! We know you're in there – come on, we need to talk."

"Just answer it, Debbie for fuck's sake. It must be important." Charlie said loud enough so whoever was at the door could hear.

They got dressed and Charlie said he would go down to the bar and get some drinks, while Debbie got rid of the girls. He opened the door and Debbie's friends from the bar came swarming in, looking Charlie up and down. He left, as the door slammed behind him and went to get a couple of beers. He had been gone about five minutes, when he made his way up to her floor. He made sure he noted the number of her door as he was turned out of it! As he got nearer, he noticed that the door was still closed and he could hear voices. But then he heard loud crying and wailing. There were the sounds of females comforting one another as he heard a girl crying and sobbing through the wood of the heavy door. Charlie, perplexed, thought *fuck this* and retired to his room with Debbie's beer and a disappointed look upon his face.

The flat moved through swiftly and the course started all too speedily for my liking. We had a couple of days to move over to Wimbledon and get settled in and cosy. That initial feeling of fear and anxiety had been replaced with an excitement and buzz of having a real place of my own. Obviously, our university house was technically my first place, but the state it was in, led me to detach myself from it a bit. This would be our place and with Bobby, I knew she would be house-proud and keep it clean, even if I didn't have the skills to.

The course was intensive and tough and even in the first few weeks we found it a tiring and draining experience. We would bicker and argue constantly, and come home from the school training period and sleep for three hours before spending the evening zombified on the sofa.

I joined the Holmes Place gym in South Wimbledon in an attempt to give myself an outlet away from Bobby. Needless to say she joined too and we ended up regularly going together.

Our schools were located near each other in Sutton, which was a little town in Surrey about five miles from Croydon. I enjoyed my school immensely, Overton Grange School it was called and it was modern and new. The people were friendly and it was clear that if I applied myself there, I could make something of myself. This was a new feeling, as in the past I had not had a great deal of academic success. So I threw myself into the course and the job which was wonderful for me. However all the time, Bobby was struggling to cope with the time we were spending apart. She would nag when we got home or get tearful when I wanted to see friends or go out somewhere. I noticed she would lose her temper at the slightest thing and in all honesty, I saw another side to her I didn't like. I wondered whether she found her course harder than me and if so, what effect this would have on her.

She had always been very academic and to struggle was not something she was used to.

I tried to assuage her anger and her reticence towards me but it seemed futile in the end because no matter what I did, it was never good enough. This worried and panicked me as I remembered the nights with my Dad, during my teenage years, listening to him tell me about his marriage problems. The main reason my parents' break up occurred, in his eyes, was that nothing he ever did or could do, would make my mother happy. I heard him say this so many times I ended up not believing it in the end. But I think he was right, because I could feel this happening to me with Bobby. Nothing I did would make her happy. So I did the only thing left. I planned a nice meal out in the centre of Wimbledon and decided to ask her to marry me. She said yes and for a brief while I felt the love drag itself back into our lives.

Charlie checked the time. It was around 4am. He went back to the room and Steve wasn't there, so he decided to go back down to the gaming floor and see where the boys were. He noticed Kevin with a vodka and coke in his hand playing on the coin machines. He looked over at the Craps tables and saw Anthony leaning over and shouting at another gambler. The situation looked like it could turn a little nasty, so Charlie went and grabbed his pal and led him out of the casino doors and into the thick desert air.

The boys took a walk up the strip and were met by a few guys trying to get them into local strip clubs. They looked at each other and smiled, 'why not?' the collective opinion was. Before they had time to collect their thoughts, they were in a limousine heading away from the centre of town.

The strip club was bathed in blue, inside and out. Charlie walked in and was amazed at the size and scale of the venue. It was circular in shape and had five different levels. Everywhere he looked there were girls waiting, smiling and gesturing; trying to find some sucker to entertain for the next half hour.

On the ground floor in front of him, Charlie saw the first dancing area where girls writhed and gyrated over horny men. The boys fancied a drink and wanted to get in the mood, so decided to go to the bar. It didn't take long before Anthony was buying drinks for four as two girls made their way over.

Charlie chatted away to his, moving away from his pal and into a dark corner. The girl was a young Mexican. She had big brown eyes and dark curly hair up in a pin. Charlie decided to humour her, enjoying the falseness of the situation and told a few stories about his life and what he was doing there. The Mexican spent a little time talking about her kids and the husband she had left before leading Charlie upstairs and to the darkest part of the casino. Charlie took some money out of his wallet and gave it to a burly man in a black suit who nodded as he walked past into another room.

Charlie realised that the room was filled with other couples who were dimly lit in the perennial blue glow. It was not the debauched and erotic scene he expected. Some were getting it on; others were just sitting and chatting, enjoying a drink and some company. If he thought about it too much Charlie would indeed find this place quite sad but he wasn't going to be brought down on his first night or morning in Las Vegas.

He sat down in the darkness with the Mexican girl. He continued to make small talk while she breathed her warmth onto his neck. He felt a little ill at ease in this sort of environment, in public, but 'when in Rome…' he thought to himself.

Charlie ended up paying over $150 at the strip club and in some respects he felt that it was money well spent. He looked back on the night with a sense of hope and excitement, despite knowing full well he had been played like every other idiot who came to Las Vegas to escape their mundane little lives. The truth was he didn't care. He knew he was going to spend the rest of his life with the woman he loved, so what was wrong with a little fantasy? Yeah, he had talked a little about going home with the Mexican and living there. They even talked in Charlie's drunken state of getting married and leaving their lives behind. She may have licked his nipple and had his full erection in her small, soft hand. But it was a moment in time and no-one need know. Charlie reflected that his life needed some excitement and fantasy, even if it was all a load of rubbish.

The good thing was Charlie had found Anthony drinking cocktails at the bar and they were ready to get themselves home.

"Did you have a good night bro?" Charlie asked tiredly, hearing his bed calling him home.

"Oh yeah, it was fun and you?" replied Anthony.

Charlie smiled at Anthony and Anthony knew as always Charlie had enjoyed himself. But before Charlie had the chance to reply, the boys felt a tap on the shoulder and feared the worst. Charlie slowly turned around expecting to see an angry doorman, but was surprised to see the Mexican and a friend she had brought out from the strip club.

"Oh, hi! How are you doing?" Charlie asked.

"We're good and wondering whether you had space in your taxi home for us two?" The Mexican replied coyly.

The two men looked at each other and smiled. Charlie could see the tiredness in Anthony's eyes but he could also feel the fire behind them. Anthony pulled the face he usually pulls when he knows he should not be doing something. He pursed his lips together and tried not to grin but it was too late as Charlie burst out laughing.

"Well, what do you reckon Ant?" Charlie asked, putting his hand on his mates shoulder.

Anthony replied, "Well I don't see why not?"

The taxi pulled up and Charlie knew there would be some difficulty getting these two girls up into the room. Late at night, the casino had doormen patrolling and anything that looked dodgy was not really welcome in the casino. Not to mention it was coming up for 6am now and these girls looked exactly like what they were, in their skinny fit dresses and layers of makeup. All around the globe, you can recognise a prostitute or a stripper just from the makeup. So they decided to go in separately, Anthony gave the girls his room number as he was staying in a room on his own. They agreed to meet them at the room ten minutes later, after having a drink.

The boys went up to the room and couldn't really contain their excitement.

"How much do you reckon this will be mate?" Charlie asked.

"Fuck knows! I tell you what though, I got 1300 dollars in that safe over there, so..."

"It can't be that much *can* it?" Charlie returned.

"Well I guess it depends on what we want, doesn't it?" Anthony beamed over at Charlie.

Fuck me, Charlie thought *that's a lot of dough*. Charlie knew he had about 1000 quid to spend on his credit card and about 300 dollars in cash in his room.

"Mate that is a lot of dough! Are you sure?" Charlie said.

"Yeah, yeah, yeah, we can sort out the money tomorrow can't we?" Anthony said. He was a generous man to say the least, but this was bordering on really stupid Charlie thought. With that there was a knock at the door.

Needless to say, Bobby wanted to get straight on with sorting out a wedding venue post haste and organised to see a few places in the heart of Kent. I went feeling a little disgruntled; that ever-present feeling of resentment sticking in the back of my throat.

We settled on a place that was like an old-fashioned Victorian detached house, with pristine gardens and a nice long driveway for the cars. We took her folks who were over the moon to hear about the engagement, to see it and they were so taken, Bobby's Dad offered to pay the deposit to secure it on the day. Bobby beamed with delight across at me, she wanted this badly. I agreed, deciding it was a good idea and putting my reticence down to cold feet and nerves and such like.

Bobby's Dad made a big point about the deposit being non-refundable. He was making a light hearted joke in a way, but in another way, nothing is ever a joke with him. There is always a side or an angle or a button that he is trying to push. In fact, the more I thought about it, the more I disliked her parents.

Her father was a sad old man really, who hung around rugby clubs on the weekend because essentially he had made no friends throughout his life. Of course they had 'couple' friends but I never really counted that as 'real' friends. They weren't the pals who would bail you out if required or be a shoulder to cry on. They were fair-weather friends. He was a slimy and overprotective man also. He made inappropriate comments to Bobby about her size when she was a perfectly normal size ten. I remember a story she once told me about her younger years.

The parents never discouraged nudity etc. in their house it was never a problem to walk from the bathroom say, to a bedroom completely naked. I found this odd at first, but then it came to light her Dad had thought of a new nickname for her, Skippy. He poked fun at her and laughed, calling her this and refusing to tell her why, 'only when she was a bit older'.

It came to light one drunken evening that he was making a reference to her pubic hair or 'bush' and had decided to nickname his daughter 'Skippy the bush kangaroo' as a joke. This was the type of guy he was, pervy and slimy to say the least.

The mother was not much better either. She had slipped in and out of depression and eating disorders throughout her life. She was a neurotic, power-mad woman. The best analysis of her came one night after my Father had met her. He said to me never to trust someone who doesn't like music. Again, I thought this an odd thing to say but there was some truth in it. Who doesn't like music? Of course, some people are more into it than others; some people only listen to certain types or genres, but to not like music at all? That was a bit strange. So I went with my Dad on this one.

I tried to put all these thoughts to the back of my mind as Bobby gathered up my hand and her Dad put his credit card into the slot machine and offered up payment to secure our wedding day, or so he thought.

The girls came in and for the first few minutes Charlie didn't really know what to do so they just had a drink and chatted to them. It could be that the girls liked them and actually weren't going to charge them. Maybe that was the case?

"Well boys, let's talk. If you want to fuck us straight in one position it is going to cost you $500 each. But...if you want to make it last a bit longer, swap us around and well, y'know...we do a few things for you it will cost more..."

"What...things..." Anthony enquired.

The Mexican girl looked up at Anthony, "Let's just say you boys will definitely have a good time..." she purred.

"How much then?" Charlie asked.

"We can say 1500 all in?" the other girl said. She was a sweet looking blonde- haired girl. She took off her shoes and lay on the spare bed, with one leg cocked as she watched my face.

"That's a lot, you know. I think too much." I replied. "What about 1000 dollars all in?" I retorted.

"What about 1250?" the Mexican whispered, stroking my cock again.

Not for the first time tonight, Anthony and I looked at each other and smiled.

"Ok then..."

20

So the future was set and all I could think about was getting out and escaping that fucking hell hole. We had a customary celebratory drink with Bobby's parents before making our way back to Wimbledon. Bobby was jubilant. All her dreams of a white wedding were coming true. This was a good time to ask for a favour.

"Honey, I got a text from some guys from work. They are going out for a few drinks tonight in Sutton, do you mind if I meet them later on?" I asked.

"Since you have made me so happy, of course you can go! Don't be *too* late home though." Bobby joked. Although it never seemed like joking when she said stuff like this.

I sniggered. "Ok. To be honest I will probably drive anyway and just have a few."

I dropped Bobby off at home, gave her a kiss and drove into Sutton. I should have really got a cab, but I just wanted to get away and in some male company as quickly as possible.

I found the pub where the guys were. Well it was two guys and two girls, all single, but I didn't bother telling Bobby that. The car was parked in the local supermarket car park and I thought that if need be I would move it to a safer place later on.

I entered the pub and said my hellos halfway through a heated conversation that was taking place.

"I just can't get over how much I like him!" stated one of the girls from work, Natalie.

"Natalie, you are supposed to be getting married!" replied Michael, one of the lads from the science department.

"I know but...his voice and...oh, I just fancy him!" she blurted out, giggling to her pal, whose name was Carrie. She was also in the science department and was well known to me already. She was one of those annoying people who have a tendency to get too drunk at every social occasion and be very loud and very obnoxious.

"Who are you talking about?" I tried to get into the conversation.

"Shh...shh...he's coming back!" whispered Natalie.

"Well, it was always going to happen sooner or later, the banks just can't keep lending here and there to everyone. It has been irresponsible." Mike covered for the gossiping girls as John, who was one of the trainees from the course and also at the same school, came to the table. Natalie looked sheepishly across at him and took a sip from her drink.

Anthony went to the safe with glee. Charlie presumed he was thinking about how the next few hours would unfold. He gave the money to the Mexican who put it in her bag and went into the bathroom to make a phone call.

"Well come here then!" the blonde girl said to Anthony, who all of a sudden became quite shy and insular.

The Mexican came out of the bathroom with an icy look on her face; her attitude had changed completely since she first entered the room. She lay down on the bed and undid her top to reveal a pair of light brown and saggy breasts. She looked at Charlie with scorn, as if to say 'well get on with it then,' but this was not what she was advertising a few minutes ago. It all seemed contrived as if she couldn't fuck off fast enough now.

She leant over to Charlie and placed his hands on her breasts. She was rough with him, but Charlie tried to ignore it and make the most of the situation. He went to undo her top, but as soon as he did, her phone started going again. She apologised and went back into the bathroom to take it.

Charlie was getting more and more aggravated and looked over at his pal. When he did, he made eye contact with Anthony, something he hoped he wouldn't do in this situation and Anthony looked worried and anxious. He was fumbling around but with little success but by this time the bathroom door had swung open and out came the other girl in nothing but her lingerie. Usually this is a good thing, but she had the air about her of a bitch who couldn't be bothered and didn't have time. Charlie was pushed down to the mattress for the second time tonight, but as she tore at his flies and yanked his jeans off, things came to a head, as the phone rang for the third time.

"What the fuck is going on? Can you not turn that fucking thing off! We have just given you over a thousand dollars!" Charlie shouted out. Anthony stood up and waited for instruction.

"Fuck you, prick! That is below the going rate in Vegas. You're lucky to even..." but before the little Mexican could finish, her friend had cut across trying to diffuse the situation.

"I am sure we can sort this out, huh? There is no need to get like that, we are here for a good time!"

"Fuck these assholes, let's get out of here." The Mexican said again.

Anthony stood motionless watching his 1200 dollars disappear before the sun came up on his first full day in Vegas. The girls went to chat in the bathroom and Charlie tried to calm himself down.

"Man, we have been fucked over here. They are going to go with my money," Anthony said.

"They are not getting out of that fucking door if they don't put out mate." Charlie replied calmly.

"Really? Who knows who the fuck they are on the phone to. There could be someone coming over to 'visit' right now." Anthony pleaded, but with that the bathroom door opened.

The blonde girl gestured to Charlie to follow her and as she did the pug-faced little Mexican girl came out and lay down next to Anthony.

Charlie went in the bathroom and the girl locked it behind her.

"We agreed to swap, probably for the best, y'know? Now how do you want it?" the blonde girl said with a deep purr to her voice. She was sexy, Charlie thought. He also felt bad that one of his best pals has been lumbered with that sour faced cow in the other room. He didn't feel guilty for long as the girl stripped Charlie bare, sat him down on the toilet and placed a rubber over his growing cock. She looked up at him and smiled and sucked his cock and his balls. Charlie could hear nothing from the other room, poor Anthony he thought. Oh well...

"How do you want it, big boy. Tell me." She said as she got up from her knees. Charlie was not big into talking during sex so he grabbed her naked ass and pulled her towards him and sat her down in his lap. She giggled before riding him slowly and loudly. After all the events of tonight, Charlie forgot how horny he was and started to feel himself getting near to climax. He pushed the girl off to try and calm himself down a bit. Then he stood up and threw her down on the bathroom side and took her from behind. She screamed, like they all do and hit the mirror in front of them so hard, Charlie worried it would break, but really it was all part of the act. As she screamed 'fuck me! fuck me!' Charlie could contain himself no longer and finished with a moan, before falling back on to the toilet seat.

"Hmm…you were good honey," the sweet girl replied as she put her underwear back on quickly.

"It's ok, you don't have to lie!" Charlie smirked.

"No really, I liked it, it was fun," she said.

"Listen, sorry about earlier. Losing my temper like that. It was bullshit." As he said that the girl flushed the toilet to make a loud noise and said,

"Don't worry. Maria – she is a bitch."

"You don't say! I just feel sorry for Anthony out there." Charlie joked with her. They both laughed before opening the door and walking into the bedroom to find Anthony lying on the bed fully clothed and 'Maria' on her phone once more.

"Looks like we better go," the blonde girl said before pecking Charlie on the cheek and saying goodbye.

As the door shut behind them, Charlie thought to himself about the night he had had and how random, strange and dangerous it had been. How did people live in this town? It was crazy. Charlie thought that he now owed Anthony nearly $700 for about five minutes of fun and an argument.

He looked over at Anthony who was still mesmerised and staring at the ceiling.

"Are you ok, Ant?" Charlie asked quietly.

"Mate, that was all my money for the whole trip. In fact it was all my money in the world." Anthony said quietly and apologetically.

"Oh…well…we can sort something tomorrow," said Charlie. "Just chill out for now and try and get some sleep." Charlie said rolling over.

"Hmmm…ok, bro." As Anthony spoke Charlie watched him, wide-eyed and fearful, staring out onto the colours of the Strip down below.

PART 3

21

The night continued well and before I knew it we had drunk about five pints. We had managed to avoid any conversation about Bobby and I was pleased about that. I knew I should feel happy that I was getting married and that life continued to move on for me, but the honest truth was that I was happier around friends and in the pub than when I was with her. I don't know, it was probably me, but I always felt in some way or other I was missing out, when were just chilling indoors and watching TV. My father reckoned it was my age and that I was too young to get married. I generally agreed with him, but once the ball had started rolling, I found it very difficult to stop it. I didn't like to hurt people or let them down so I just went with things, although in this moment of clarity I was having, I knew this was not the sort of time to be rolling with the punches. Anyway, what will be I thought will be, as I looked down at my empty glass.

"Another round guys?" I asked. I had already bought one but it was my turn again soon and quite frankly I would rather get them in than wait for slowcoaches. I went to the bar and then realised as I pulled my wallet out, my car key. I still had to park the bloody thing up somewhere!

I bought the pints and decided that after this one, I would go and move it and put it in a backstreet. I looked at my watch, 9.40pm. That's fine I thought, enough time to drive the car and get it somewhere safe, before the police are out looking for arseholes like me to nick.

The rest of the Las Vegas trip passed fairly tamely in comparison to that first night. Charlie woke up though the following morning to the sound of Anthony hyperventilating and pacing the floor. It turned out that it really was Anthony's last load of money in the whole world.

Charlie avoided questions like 'why the fuck would you spend your last pennies on prostitutes?' as he thought that was probably the last thing he needed to hear.

Due to the daily cash withdrawal limits, Charlie paid Anthony back over the course of the next two days and the $700 saw him through, until the end of the stag do. Charlie was pleased as it had all the ingredients of a proper stag do. Plus, when people asked him what he did for it, they were always impressed when he said 'Las Vegas'. He worried that to this day, Anthony still felt pangs of regret about going on the holiday, but the rest of the lads really enjoyed it and they planned at some stage to go again.

He never understood people who wanted to go down the pub with their mates for their stag. If it was going to be the last of the debauchery, Charlie wanted to tackle it full steam ahead and he had.

However, the boys thought it better for the rest of the trip to steer clear of females of any kind, except of course strippers who reared their heads a few more times. No-one really knew what happened to Debbie and what upset her so much. In the long run though Charlie felt he was glad not to have fucked her. She was the sort of girl he could end up falling for and that would not have been wise. Plus there would have been comeback at home and in his heart of hearts he didn't want to cheat on Jo. With the prostitutes he never felt so bad because there was no emotional attachment, it was purely physical and thus Charlie could rationalise it as not being so bad. He doubted Jo would agree, but what she didn't know would never hurt her.

Charlie returned home bruised and battered from an orgy of drinking. In fact he and his mate Heath were extremely drunk when they boarded the plane home. Heath nearly had a fight with a chap in the airport, while Charlie just slowly sobered up and felt more and more ill as the journey wore on. He was glad to be going home though as he missed Jo throughout the trip, even if his actions didn't reflect his thoughts.

She was there at Gatwick to meet him and she flung herself towards him with open arms when he arrived from baggage claim. He got to the car exhausted, but relieved that life for the meantime could return to normal somewhat.

"I don't care, I'm getting shots!" declared the already drunk Carrie. I wasn't that bothered though really as I had the taste for the booze now and was keen to have more. Moving the car had gone out of the window as an idea, three more pints had gone down and last orders were about to be called.

Carrie got five shots of sambuca which in all honesty were not that tasty but did the trick for Carrie, to say the least. As she got up to leave the pub for a cigarette, she fell to the floor. Prompting hysterical laughter from Jon and I. Carrie snarled up at us, her skin was greasy and blotchy from far too much booze and mumbled something under her breath. Before we could reply, Mike and Natalie had scooped her up under each sweaty armpit, said their goodbyes and made for the taxi rank.

I downed my beer fairly quick as the pub was looking to close. I said goodbye to Jon who went after the others and over the road to the taxi rank. I waited outside letting the cool night air fill my lungs. It was true what they said about stepping outside after a drink it makes you realise how drunk you are!

I checked my phone to see if anyone had rung and found a text message on the phone from Bobby. *We need to talk when you get back.* No kisses? I thought it best to ring her back.

"Hi hun its me I am 'bout to get a taxi home. What's up?" I asked jovially.

"You are a wanker. That is what's up." She replied in her stern tone.

I giggled. "Yeah I know that, but only when you are not around!" I tried to lighten the mood, but it was to no avail.

"Fuck off, I found out about one of your little slags from university," she continued.

"Wha...I..."

"Yeah. Jen, is it? Emailing your hotmail account – wanting to apologise and...you know, I don't know why I even bother with you, fuck you. I have had enough!" she said, slamming the phone down.

I tried to call her back a few times. I even tried the house phone but it wasn't happening. I had to see her and quickly because when in a rage like this, she had the potential to do anything.

I took my car key and stared at it. I am not even that pissed, I thought. I feel fine. The air has sobered me up a bit and to be honest, it is not far down the road.

I ran up to the car park, got in the car and started the engine. I tried far too hard not to draw attention to myself. I took the back roads but ended up down streets I didn't know. I wanted to get onto a main road and get to a sign post. I carried on driving until I found one that said Sutton or Carshalton. I knew I didn't want to go back to Sutton so I took the road to Carshalton. It was a nice village actually with old brick walls and little pubs and so on. I could feel myself rushing inside; I didn't feel well. I came to a mini roundabout and carried straight on towards Carshalton Village...It was a nice place, I thought looking straight ahead at a big, old-fashioned pub with white wash walls and orange lights brightening up the night. What was it called? I squinted and looked closer to see. The Grey...the grey something and then before I could focus, all I heard was a massive thud and I felt the car pulling me to my left. What the fuck was going on? I looked at the speedometer and saw I was doing close to 40m.p.h. but I had lost control of the car and it was veering, quickly into a lake. I tried to slam on the brakes but they had failed and the car clipped the side of the road, went through a metal chain, flipped on its side and into the lake. Everything around me went black as I closed my eyes.

22

Charlie and Jo arrived at their wedding venue, the Farnham Castle, early on Thursday morning. They were due to marry on the Friday and wanted to make sure they got there in plenty of time for the wedding practise and to make sure the final arrangements were in place. That is not to say that they were the first to arrive as Jo's parents had arrived a few hours earlier. The weather had been poor for August. In fact summer 2008 was one of the worst summers on record, although the sun had popped out briefly that day. Jo was getting stressed about the weather, so Charlie thought it best to keep to himself the fact that showers were forecast tomorrow.

Charlie and his ushers went to a pub for lunch. The pub was only a short walk from the Castle and it was a pleasant walk down the hill to it. The sun was shining now and bathed the open road in light. The pub was small and cosy with a fire burning in the corner. The seats were made of solid oak and the lager was cold and fresh, how it should be. This was a far cry from the trendy bars they were used to and a welcome change. Too often the lager was warm and the service was cold, at significantly higher prices as well.

The boys ate heartily as they knew the afternoon would be hard work. Suit fittings were required in the first instance in the Moss Brothers shop in town. They also had to erect three gazebos on the lawn, outside the castle, before making their way over to the church for a run through of the ceremony. It was one of those days which passed quickly and although they had plenty of tasks to complete, it was fun because they knew they had so much to look forward to tomorrow.

After the practise ceremony, they were able to relax and planned to have a big meal at one of the local restaurants in town. Pretty much all of the main players had arrived for the wedding, so the older folks went to Café Rouge, whilst the younger group headed to Zizzi's restaurant. Charlie was pleased and excited with the way things were going and was trying hard not to drink too much before tomorrow. He wanted to be on top form for the most important day of his life.

They chatted warmly with their closest friends and finalised the little details and as the meal came, Charlie paid as a 'thank you' to all his friends for making the effort of coming down a day before and helping out.

Jo, being more sensible, decided to turn in and kissed her fiancé good night. She left to go back to the castle with her maid of honour and a few of the bridesmaids. Charlie finished his wine, before a few of his pals suggested a night cap in the pub.

The boys had a few more relaxing drinks and some of the bridesmaids and family members came to join them. It was a lovely time for all, except maybe the best man Steve, who was fretting about his potentially undercooked speech.

At about midnight they made their way back up the hill to the beauty and majesty of the castle rooms. Charlie, who was rooming with Steve and Charlie in anticipation of the day ahead, tried to get to sleep straight away to feel fresh for the morning. Steve worked hard on getting his speech right. Charlie couldn't sleep properly though, as he was far too excited about the day in store. He didn't mind the tossing and turning as he was almost certain Jo was doing exactly the same too, across the hotel, in another room somewhere.

Through the darkness, I heard my car door opening and the voice of a stranger.

"Fucking hell, you all right mate?" it said, as an arm reached in to pull me out. I came to and realised what had just happened. What should I do? Run for it? There was a crowd gathering to see the wreckage. I turned back towards to the car and saw steam rising from the bonnet. The damage to the front made it almost unrecognisable. I was a lucky boy. I heard sirens ringing and immediately started to panic. I thought it best to dive into the cover of the pub opposite the road. The Greyhound it was called, I could see now. The adrenaline was flying through my veins and I was panicking. I thought maybe if I could get a pint of coke or water it may sober me up?

I made my way to the pub door, only to be stopped by two police men getting out of a car in the car park.

"Excuse me sir, is that your car?"

Oh fuck, I thought. What have I done?

23

Charlie woke up and immediately checked the weather outside. It was a scary wait as the curtain opened. Grey cloud, but a bit of brightness and thankfully no rain! Steve was comatose as the alarm went off so Charlie used the bathroom before him. He put the kettle on to boil while he was washing. His bathroom window overlooked the castle courtyard and Charlie couldn't quite believe how far he had come. More importantly, he was happy with where he was. He had no qualms about getting married to Jo and no cold feet. He remembered talking to his father about marriage and his father showing him a picture as Mum and he left the church. His hand was curled up into a fist and you could tell by the veins on his hand that he was clenching it tight. He said that was fear and frustration because he was so scared at the thought of it all. What a pussy, Charlie thought.

He had bought all the best toiletries and proceeded to wash himself over four times. Charlie had a few drinks last night, nothing major, but what he really hated was the smell of alcohol ruminating off someone's body after a night out. So he made sure he was as fresh as could be. He had a nice tan from the summer months, but he made sure to compliment it with a drop from a bottle too. He got his hair in his favourite style and mouth washed three times before leaving the bathroom.

"Fucking hell, I thought you had fallen asleep in there," said Steve as he jumped in the bathroom after me.

"Not likely! Right, quickly we have 20 minutes until photos!" Charlie said as he got his suit out of the wardrobe.

"Yeah, it is."

"We are going to have to breathalyse you. That's the law, I'm afraid."

"Ok, no problem. Can I get a soft drink from in the pub? I am a bit shaky."

"Yep, we'll be out here, when you're ready."

I was beginning to panic now. There were three doors in and out of the pub. I reckon I could make a run for it; there is a church and cemetery around the back. Surely I could get out that way? But, there was no point as that was my car hanging out of the lake over the road, so they would be able to find me. I ordered a pint of diet coke and took out a 2p coin and started to suck on it. Someone once told me it affects the breathalyser and stops it working. It was worth a shot. I downed my diet coke and wondered if in some way it may help the situation. I tried to assess my options but before I could make a decision, the copper was peering through the door and motioning me to come out. I went and faced the music.

"Ok, you just need to breathe into this." He said holding out what looked like one of those old Lucozade cartons. I took the plastic spout in my mouth.

"Take a deep breath and breathe out as steadily as you can." He said slowly.

"Ok." I took a deep breath and felt a strange surge of anxiety fill my chest and stomach. Pins and needles ran up and down my arms and my vision blurred to black before I hit the ground and was out for the second time tonight.

Steve and Charlie were late for the photos, but it was not a major concern as the weather had held out and they managed to get a few good ones of the boys pinning on each other's flowers and some of Charlie standing in a doorway in a catalogue-style pose. Charlie was not overly fussed as he thought the photos of the morning were generally geared around the bride. As long as she had good ones of Jo, that was what mattered.

He had kept to his promise of not contacting her at all on the day. He did text her good night at about half past midnight when he got in, but he thought that that could be forgiven.

The photos were done and the main banquet hall was set up, so the boys got in their cars and headed down to the church. Just up the road from it was a little country pub that had just opened. Charlie and Steve popped in for a traditional livener and were pleased to find a lot of their friends and day guests already in there. He got chatting, while the ushers went to the church and Charlie found himself relaxing nicely into the day. The truth was, he took quite nicely to being the centre of attention and talked lucidly and jovially, killing time before the service started and his bride arrived.

The bumps on the road awoke me. It looked like I had been put into one of those big police vans. But they hadn't put me in the main part, where the real criminals go. I was shut in the 3 foot wide space at the entrance to the back of the van. The alcohol was wearing off and I was beginning to feel quite sick with the movement of the van. We finally made it to the police station and I heard the coppers stop the van and get out. As they unlocked the back of the van, I heard them talking to each other loudly about how they could smell alcohol on my breath. What a bunch of wankers, I hate the police I thought. They never did things in a simple and helpful way. There always had to be some form of piss-taking or intimidation.

It had transpired that I had passed out while trying to take the breathalyser, possibly of delayed shock from the accident. They had decided that I was going to give a blood sample instead but I had to wait for the on-call doctor to arrive which could be at anytime of the night. So after a bit of paperwork, they threw me in one of their holding cells. It was quite an experience, hearing that thick metal door shut behind me. The room was small, claustrophobic and cold. There was a wooden rectangle with a slim mattress on it and a dirty pillow. A toilet sat in one corner and that was it.

I began to panic and sweat. I could be here all night! I started banging on the metal door, panicked, but no-one came. I started doing press ups and sit ups in a vain and foolish attempt to burn some of the alcohol flowing through my system. I even drank some of the water from the toilet bowl as I was so thirsty and no one was coming to find out what I wanted. I felt sick and anxious so tried to lie down and close my eyes, but the room spun and spun, I rolled over and prayed for sleep.

24

In true Jo-style she was 45 minutes late to the ceremony. But despite this and the guests getting a little bored and anxious the service ran smoothly. Jo looked lovely as Charlie knew she would, but he was an odd creature and preferred her less made up and more natural. Nevertheless, she did look spectacular and the beaming grin across her face and the tears of joy sweeping down her face meant so much to Charlie, as he fumbled his way nervously through the ceremony.

The church was magnificently decked out with pink ribbons and roses decorating the pews. The organ stood tall and proud, while the choir (despite looking a little tired and forlorn with the wait) added to the splendour of the ritual.

After the wedding ceremony and photos, Charlie and Jo took a well deserved break in the form of a drive around the Surrey countryside. The sun had come out fully and bathed the little country roads and wide green fields in hot sunshine. Charlie and Jo kissed and chatted about the wonder of the day so far, whilst sipping on champagne, relaxing as their driver ferried them around in an old-fashioned Rolls Royce.

Arriving back at the castle after the guests, they had an opportunity to chat to their friends and families while listening to the jazz band, specifically chosen by Charlie's father in law. They were a twee affair, with little straw hats and stripy red blazers.

The grounds looked elegant and well-maintained and the sun shone down all afternoon as if some eternal power was giving its own blessing on this union. Jo for one couldn't be happier. Charlie was happy, but was starting to get aggravated by the amount of photos that needed to be taken. He was getting tetchy and even a kiss from his lover's mouth was not quelling his angst.

However, he grinned and bore it knowing that a pint of lager in a little while would begin to ease his qualms.

The rest of the day passed with ease and delight for the revellers at the castle. Steve and Charlie's speech went down very well and Jim's speech was heartfelt and thoughtful.

During the meal, Charlie imbibed far more than he should have, he was incredibly nervous about talking sincerely in front of all these people and as soon as Steve had finished his speech, he went outside for some fresh air and a cigarette. To say he felt a little tipsy at this point was an understatement. Fuck it, he thought, it is my day.

The evening passed with fervour and excitement. More revellers arrived for the evening and they were truly entertained with an array of events. There was a chocolate fountain, the customary disco and a surprise firework display to mark the culmination of the night's entertainment.

Charlie and Jo left hand in hand to their honeymoon suite, with a wave of applause accompanying them and good will comments and gestures resonating in their ears. Their union was sanctified and they both felt truly as if not only their friends and families hearts were with them but also as if the will of the Gods was too.

Charlie opened the door to his suite and carried his bride over the threshold. He was delighted to find their four-poster bed sprinkled with rose petals. Charlie lay Jo on the bed as she smiled and gazed adoringly up at her man.

The metal door clanked open and I was summoned out. I felt slightly more sober as I met the doctor who was going to take my blood. I was ushered into a little room at the side of the station and was asked questions about what I had done that night and about my medical history. The doctor took the blood and gave me a sample to take in a little jar. The needle was cold and icy as it drove through my skin. I was signed out of the station and retrieved my personal belongings before being pointed towards freedom.

As I stepped out into Sutton high street, a wave of panic hit my stomach; I hadn't spoken to Bobby. I checked my phone and there were no missed calls. Strange? I tapped in her number and waited for her voice. She answered straight away and seemed tearful.

"Hello."

"Hey, sorry I haven't called. I have got some bad news..." I started out.

"I know, I heard. One of my friends saw you...they..." with that she burst into tears.

"It's ok...I'll come home." I tried to comfort her. I thought this is rich; I am the one who feels like shit and has been locked away for the night and she is the ne playing hard done by!

The phone went dead as I started the long walk home, trying not to shed a tear.

Charlie woke up to find rose petals stuck on all parts of his large frame. He looked over at Jo who was beginning to stir and mumble sweetly in her sleep. He got out of bed and headed to the bathroom for a shower, admiring the dark oak finish of the bathroom door and the quality of the work that lay inside. Despite his error- strewn life, he felt as if events were turning around. When something good was happening in his life, he felt like he deserved it and finally saw a way out of drinking and depression for good, with Jo.

In the past, Charlie had always assumed he would follow in the footsteps of his father, who despite his many lovers, never seemed to find happiness with a woman. He assumed that his flirtations with alcoholism would lead to greater addiction and depths of despair, that finally he would be end up as a drunk in the local Wetherspoons, awaiting its opening at 11am and quaffing down sherry before midday. He always envisaged having friends of some description, fellow drunks or wasters and he always thought he would be able to find some solace in the bottom of a bottle. It had worked for his Dad for years and his father before him, but here in the honeymoon suite in Farnham Castle, Charlie felt a different sensation. He looked at his glowing reflection in the mirror and he saw a man who could succeed.

As Charlie grew up, he felt like he wanted to *be* his Father, live the same life and ignore the costs. Be a free spirit and live by the libertine code until his dying day, not caring who got hurt or destroyed along the way. Now, he looked in the mirror and saw a man who was loved and didn't want to hurt those that loved him. He thought of his wife and his dear mother who had supported him all the way. He looked in the mirror and saw someone who could do more than his father did. It was the first day he had ever felt that feeling.

25

I grabbed the big U2 coffee book from the bedroom and laid it out flat on the coffee table. It was the best book for carving up a rock on as it was entirely black on the outside cover. I pulled the plastic bag out of my jeans pocket and pulled out the white crystalline rock. It was pretty good stuff looking at it, so I leant over to the cabinet and pulled out a pack of Stanley knife blades to cut it up. Usually, I didn't buy eighths of coke, but in recent months I felt rather than keep having to score throughout the week it made more sense just to get one bag for the whole week, or in some cases two a week. It saved money in the long run I was sure. I loved doing the first line off a rock because you know you had loads so you could afford to be generous. I carved out a large line for myself and a smaller line for later. I did the first one making sure to hold my breath at the end and hold my nose, in case there was any blood. Thankfully this time there wasn't, so I got up went to the bar and fixed a large vodka and tonic, to wash the taste out of my mouth.

I turned on the TV to keep occupied. It was only a shitty one as Bobby had decided she *desperately* needed the 28" in her new pad. It felt like I was being petty if I insisted on having it, after all her Dad did buy it for us so it is more hers than mine I guess.

I looked at the calendar waiting for the buzz to kick in. It had been two months since Bobby and I had broken up and I felt I was doing ok given the nature of the break up. The night I came home from the police station she had stayed up in the front room and I saw her eyes wide and body numb, fixated on the TV as I entered. I knew it would not be easy for me, I felt so embarrassed, but as we started to talk about the events, it appeared I clearly wasn't as embarrassed as her. She broke down in tears, telling me she couldn't be with me. She was disappointed about the type of person I was becoming and so on. She had decided to end the relationship at least that is what she thought she had decided. Not wanting to cause any additional problems, I left the flat immediately and phoned one of my friends to stay with him.

Since then, I have managed to get my own place which is modest and small to say the least, but it is better than not having a place at all. Bobby has been back in contact and we meet up to fuck occasionally. I am not sure if she sees it like I do, but being away from her has changed my perspective a lot on our relationship.

I noticed I was chewing the gum faster and my mouth couldn't focus on the TV screen anymore. I didn't even know what I was watching, just something to drown out the silence and fear.

I was getting antsy, when my phone started ringing from the bedroom. I raced through to answer it.

"Hello?"

"All right mate, how you doing?"

It was my pal Anthony. "Oh, hi mate! Good. Just chilling out watching a bit of TV. What are you doing?"

"Well, I know it's early, but do you fancy a beer mate? The pub opens in half an hour." Anthony enquired eagerly.

"What's the time?" I asked, not really caring.

"Err, it is 10.20 mate." He replied.

I was beginning to sweat now. "Yeah definitely, come and pick me up!"

"No worries mate."

It had been a few months since the wedding and Charlie and Jo were still very much in love. They had moved out of Charlie's flat and into a beautiful house off the high street in Purley. For Charlie, he felt as if he had 'made it.' For a young man from the area he was from, all he wanted to do was move to Surrey and make a name for himself. He had a bit of disposable cash, he was married to a beautiful woman and he had made it into the dream. He giggled to himself as he thought that the person he was six years ago would hate him for being such a sell out and in all honesty it did still wrangle with him a tiny bit. However his feelings of contentment and his shock at ending up where he had, outweighed that significantly. He was well aware he was no Richard Branson but he was happy with himself, which he hadn't been for a very long time.

"Charlie, grab the vegetables out of the fridge," Jo demanded.

"Ok, sweetie," Charlie said mocking her tone.

"Sorry darling, it's just we have quite a lot to do before our parents get here at 4pm." She stroked his arm. "I didn't mean to snap."

"No worries. What do you want me to do?" Charlie was not often this helpful, but he felt bad as he was a lazy so and so and very rarely contributed. Jo looked around at the kitchen and said, "I will be honest with you, it would be much easier for me if you just went out for a couple of hours so I can get the cleaning done and finish the food."

Charlie couldn't believe his luck. "Are you sure babe?" he asked dutifully.

"Yes! Bugger off and go and meet Anthony down the pub! But be back before 3.30pm."

Charlie felt a wave of excitement shudder through his body as he grinned and reached for his mobile. Life could be an awful lot worse he thought to himself.

"Another lager, chief?" Anthony asked.

"Yeah, why not? I might chuck a sickie tomorrow, fuck it!" I retorted.

It was a Sunday afternoon and I had been on the powder and booze since I had woken up. I was feeling good, I always did when I was out. I had good friends, they stand by me usually or at least say the right things to me when I needed to hear them. At the moment just Jon and Anthony were out and we had been out for most of the day. They were both sporting fairly large hangovers from Saturday night. I would be too, however the cocaine had gone a long way to clearing the blues away for me.

"Yeah? What about the kids? Who is going to teach them?" Anthony asked tentatively.

"They'll be all right. Deputy Head will get some cover guy in to sit with them for the day." I slurred back.

"Will...will they be learning do you think?" Anthony asked.

"Fuck them Anthony, they are thick as shit anyway, they don't deserve an education!"

Anthony looked at me then looked away and focused his eyes away on the football showing on the TV screen.

I couldn't leave it though; I was beginning to feel hammered, as

Anthony passed me another beer, "what's the problem Ant? Has the *electrician*, got a moral problem with what I am doing? Come on, say it if you have a problem pal!" I goaded him.

"No problem mate, just interested that's all. You are your own man you make your own decisions," Anthony retorted calmly.

"Well, what is that supposed to mean? If you have a problem, say it mate."

"There's no problem chief, just calm down!" Anthony implored.

"Listen mate you're just a fucking mug, don't tell me what is right and wrong, you cunt!" I felt the anger rise inside myself and I got up from my chair.

"Calm down...you're going to get us kicked out..." Jon pleaded.

"Fuck you two!" I shouted as I threw my stool across the bar and pushed Anthony from his seat. I had no idea what was going through my head. Anthony looked at me, but before he could say anything I had turned on my heel and stormed out of the pub and into the cold night air.

26

"So come on then who do you think is the best batsman of our generation, Charlie?" Anthony asked after Jon had just mocked him for giving his answer of Sachin Tendulkar. Good shout, Charlie thought, but not the best he had seen.

"Well, it's hard isn't it? I mean I like Viv Richards, but the best? Probably...Brian Lara. He was out of this world!" Charlie said.

"Yeah, that's a good one," Jon said in support.

"Hmm, really..?" Anthony asked.

The battle raged on between the two and had they had all day, it would probably continue for long after. However, Charlie was conscious of the time as it was coming up to a quarter to four and he didn't want to upset Jo before they had their parents around for dinner.

Charlie made his excuses before leaving for home. He remembered a time he used to feel so angry and reticent about leaving his friends but now he felt fairly relaxed about it, he thought it was just another rite of passage as they moved ever closer to their thirties. Anthony was changing too. No longer was he gadding about town until three in the morning. He had responsibilities: a home, a missus. We had to change, to keep everybody happy. A lot of our younger friends say to us that they would never change themselves or adapt for any woman etc. etc. but when we hear that, we just smile at each other and think of ourselves five years ago saying exactly the same things.

It's true what they say that when you walk outside of the pub the drunkenness really hits you. I wandered for about fifteen minutes, down the dark and lonely streets, fuelled with anger, although not really understanding what had happened. I really fancied another line, so needed a quiet ledge or a cubicle of some description. I didn't want to go back to the pub and sit on my own, so I decided to ring Anthony and call a truce. He didn't answer. I tried Jon, no luck either. In the end I figured they would still be sat in the bar at the pub, feeling bad about what had happened, so I decided to head back there.

I walked in the door and it was warm and cosy. My cheeks flushed and I looked around for my friends. They were nowhere to be seen. The barman looked at me nervously so I just stared him out. They had really gone and left me on my own? This cannot be right; they wouldn't do that, would they?

The toilet was to my left and I decided to use it while I was here for a quick sniff. I went into the cubicle and locked it, unpacking my bits on the window sill opposite. As I rustled around, I heard a knock on the door. I panicked. What if it was the landlord or the Old Bill?

"Don't worry, mate it's all right just open up," an unfamiliar voice said.

I hid my powder and so on behind an old glade air freshener and proceeded to nervously open the door. In front of me, stood a big, burly red-haired man. I knew him from the local pubs. I think he was a builder by trade, but he had a reputation for being a bit of a football thug and a dealer in our area.

He looked at me and smiled, "hello son, you don't know me, but I know what you have been up to all day in here." He smiled.

What, what are you on about I was just..." I nervously retorted.

"It's ok pal, you have been in and out of the bog all day. I know what you have been doing." He said confidently, as he pulled an enormous clear bag out of his pocket and laid it on the side. He opened it up and it must have had at least 3/4 of a gram of coke in it. He emptied it out and onto the window sill. He saw my paraphernalia behind the air freshener and smirked at me.

"Chances are you got that gear off me," he said in a loud, unfriendly voice. He didn't care who heard us, the cubicle door was unlocked and punters could see quite clearly that there were two blokes in there.

"If you didn't, you will do next time, ok?" he said as he snorted a massive line.

I nodded vigorously, as he gave me a card with a name and number on it. He gestured to me to finish the rest of his gear on the window sill, which really was more than generous. I didn't know whether he was testing me, but then he put his rolled up £10 note in my hand and walked out of the toilet. I stared at the big pile in front of me and thought, it would be rude not to, so I did the whole lot.

I wandered out of the toilet and into the brightness of the pub. The gear had hit me hard, it was really powerful stuff. I was sweating and swaying under the bright lights I noticed the mysterious guy across the bar, talking to a large group of friends. He looked at me and nodded. With that a wave of panic came over me and I left the pub and made my way home. I went to the bus stop but thought I would be lucky to get one at this time on a Sunday night. I began the walk to where I lived. It didn't feel right calling it a home the way I felt at the moment.

I decided to call Bobby and see what she was doing.

"Hey, where are you?" I asked coolly.

"I am at home of course where you should be. What are you doing?" she asked abruptly.

"Well, I am on my *way* home; I had just been for a few beers. Do you want to come over?" I asked.

"No, I don't think so. It's getting late." She replied.

"I know. Well I thought I would take tomorrow off and just lay in bed, if you fancied it?" Bobby worked at a private school and so had longer holidays than the rest of the teaching world. I knew she was off the next day and would probably say yes.

"No, I don't think it is a good idea I'm just beginning to get my head around all the things that have happened..." she said softly.

"oh, ok...it is just that I...miss you, but don't worry, you're probably right..." I agreed.

Silence on the other end of the line. I waited to see what she would do. The great thing about being so high and drunk is you never really felt guilty for the problems you caused. I knew this was a terrible idea. I knew I had fallen out of love with Bobby and she was still in love with me.

"Ok, I'll be there in twenty minutes, see you then!" the phone went dead.

I smiled to myself as I entered the flat, heart pounding with excitement and greed. I took out my drugs and put them on the side ready for another line after I had fixed a couple of drinks. That was the thing about cocaine. It made you feel invincible. Not only that, it took all of your feelings and emotions out of the equation; left on the shelf to worry about when you came down. At the moment I felt that time would not come. I had a steady income, a good job and no responsibilities or ties. That's how I felt; although karma had a different plan for me.

27

The parents came around for late lunch and all the trimmings were prepared. The table was laid out with candles, napkins and crystal glasses. While Jo prepared the last of the food, Charlie with a rekindled joviality, made a toast and entertained the guests. The afternoon went well and after much wine and merriment, the party fizzled out and the folks decided it was time to retire home. Jo kissed them goodbye at the door while Charlie walked his and her mother to their respective cars.

"Now you look after her son, she is so very good to you don't you know?" announced Charlie's mother as she kissed him goodbye.

Charlie nodded tiredly, thinking of all the times he had heard words to this effect over the course of his life. He wondered whether anyone ever said it to his respective partners over the years.

"Yes Mother that is why I married her!" he laughed, as she muttered words under her breath.

As their cars pulled away, Charlie stood in the open doorway and looked up and down his street. The streetlights were buzzing with electricity and shone their dim yellow glow onto the pavement as they warmed up. Charlie breathed a sigh of relief at the end of an exhausting afternoon.

As feelings of contentment washed over him, at a successful afternoon and a relaxing evening to follow, where he would probably share a bottle of wine and settle down to a film with his wife, he noticed something worrying in the distance. Two shapes were fighting and arguing near the alleyway.

As he squinted to get a better look, he could see a man following a girl and pushing her up against a fence. She tried to push him away, but as she did he grabbed her arms hard and slapped her hard across the face. She let out a little yelp, before the man put his hand to her throat and pushed her body up against the wall.

Charlie couldn't allow this to happen. His instincts took over and he ran towards the man. As he did, he saw him force his hand up the woman's skirt and into her tights. Anger took over and Charlie started shouting at the man as he sprinted towards him. The man didn't even turn around, but he fled up the alleyway and over a wall. Charlie, full of rage now, continued after him. He couldn't see where he had gone but scaled the wall and continued across the garden in front of him. He could hear the sounds of footsteps, but there were no footprints. The guy was long gone,

He decided to head back to the alleyway and see if the girl was all right. Much to his surprise as he got there, she too was nowhere to be found.

His heart fluttered as he remembered his wide open front door with the light pouring out and Jo probably innocently washing up, expecting him to be there, to be protecting her from the world outside and all its ills.

Charlie hurried back around the corner and looked into the distance, noticing the light had gone from the living room of the house. He sprinted back, shouting his wife's name pleading for her to answer, but to no avail.

As he burst through the door, the lights were all off; in fact it appeared all the electricity was. He ran through the house calling Jo's name. There was no answer. She was nowhere to be found.

28

I awoke with a lump in the bed next to me. I wasn't a hundred percent sure who it was, so I quietly moved the quilt from in front of my face and through bleary eyes I saw the face of Bobby peacefully in front of me. With her eyes shut and not talking, she could be quite sweet I thought.

My head was banging hard so I got up and went to the kitchen to fix some water and ibuprofen. I didn't really remember much after Bobby arrived. I did remember arguing with Anthony though; I needed to sort that out today. I was off my head and although I don't remember the ins and the outs, it was almost certain I was in the wrong. As I drank the water, which felt like life blood to my aching body, Bobby emerged in the doorway.

"Hey. How are you feeling?" she asked coldly.

"Ok," I lied. "Why?"

"Do you not remember last night?" she asked.

"Yeah, I remember you arriving and..."

"Yeah and? Do you not remember anything else? A fight perhaps?" she asked.

"Look, I'm sorry. I was wasted...I had a row with Anthony...I was a bit all over the place..." I tried to calm her down.

"Not with me Charlie, with the guy from next door! You threatened to cut him up, you were so...so..." she was lost for words. Did that happen? I do remember something occurring...I think he knocked on the door and I sent him away.

"What happened then?" I asked tentatively.

"What does it matter? You always do the same things don't you? Fuck up all the time, get drunk just like your Father, just like you..."

"Oh thanks, Bobby! Then why the fuck are you here if I am such an arsehole? Why do you come around at midnight if you can't bear to look at me or be with me?" I shouted back.

"Because part of me *hoped* you would change. Would see what you are missing and *change*. But in fact, you're getting worse!"

"Why do you think I am like this, Bobby? Why do you think I do the things I do? Do you think it is because I feel loved and supported? Do you think it is because *you* make me happy?" I retorted. My head was spinning; I didn't want to hurt her anymore than I had. I don't know why I even allowed her to come over anymore. What ever we had was now gone. Our relationship was in tatters and every now and again, Bobby would gather all the pieces and try and sow them back together again.

"Look, Bobby...I don't want to hurt you..."

"Oh, fuck off Charlie! If you cared about me, if you even had some feelings for me, you would be trying to make things better, trying to change, to *impress* me! But you're not! You care more about your fucking friends than you do me!" she screamed.

"Bobby. I have tried to tell you many, many times before, this has run its course...it's over...we don't work..." I trailed off. I bored myself with how many times I had repeated this over and over again.

"Well...I don't want to give up on you...we can still make it work... we..." she was desperate. Clawing at some fairytale. A romantic notion in her head that could never be realised. She grabbed me and tried to kiss me. I felt nothing in my heart but pity and emptiness. I let her kiss me and as she became more heated, her actions felt more sinister. She pushed me onto the sofa and grabbed for my cock in my pants. She tore at my clothes and kissed me harder and harder until I couldn't bear it any longer.

"Get off, Bobby! This is wrong!" I felt a sudden urge to get out, to push her away. She landed on the floor in a heap. She started crying and sobbing, pitifully moaning.

"Charlie...why don't you want me?"

"I have had enough of this. I am sick of being judged by you all the time. Yes, I drink too much, yes I take too many drugs, but I am not as bad as you make out!"

"But it is such a mess, Charlie..." she pleaded.

"Bobby, *you* are such a mess. You need to leave me alone, I can't take this anymore. Things would be fine; I could get my life under control, if you let us end this, it is dangerous and unsafe. I am warning you, if we continue to see each other like this things are going to get worse, get dangerous. It is not you or me that is wrong. It is this relationship, we need to stop it!"

I wasn't sure where all this was coming from but I knew what I was saying was right. It was like a drug and we were addicts. We loved each other and people often thought that was all you needed, that you could work around all other problems if you had love. But that was not always the case. In a moment of clarity, I could see the future and how things would pan out if we stayed together.

"But, I love you..."

Jo was never found. The police came to the house and could find very little evidence of anything to go on. They presumed that the 'attack in the alleyway' was some sort of decoy, maybe, to lure Charlie out of the house. Charlie had assured them that it was someone that he knew, someone from his past who had a grudge against him. He gave them her name, they investigated it, they took her in for questioning, but it turned out she had an alibi for that time on that Saturday. They asked him what was the purpose of leaving his house and his wife? Why didn't he just ring the police? To this, Charlie had no answer. He could only guess it was instinct.

Charlie asked them whether his wife would ever be found. They said it was unlikely, but to stay positive. Charlie thought that was an interesting way to think. He told the police he was adamant it was Helen and that this was some sick plot she had masterminded. They told Charlie he needed to calm down and that there was no evidence for that. No evidence? There may not have been *evidence*, but in his heart, he knew. He asked if there was anything to go on? No fingerprints, footprints? They said the rain that fell at dusk on the Saturday had washed all of them away.

My head was spinning from the drama with Bobby. I needed to get out of there, I didn't care what she did or where she went, *I* just needed to be gone from that place. I showered and got changed, my actions still frantic and inconsistent. I came out of the bedroom and thankfully Bobby had gone, but the room was still a mess. There were broken cups on the floor and my upturned coffee table in the middle of the room.

On the kitchen side, Bobby had left a note. It read, '*we need to talk under different circumstances, can we meet tomorrow at 1pm? I'll pick you up. Let's not end it like this.*' I tore up the note and thought no more of it. Like fuck was I meeting her tomorrow.

I left the mess for later and decided to walk into Sutton. I knew a few of my friends were at the Treasury and although I wasn't massively keen on getting hammered, the thought of sitting around in the flat, dwelling on things, did not appeal at all.

It was a fairly long walk, through the backstreets of the poet's area and across Benhill Park. I willed the grey despondent clouds to shed out their drizzle and rain in the vain hope they could wash away this bloody mess I had made.

I walked up the high street to the bar and realised that time had really gotten away from me, evening was drawing in and the bars were looking fairly busy as I passed them. I felt like talking to a girl tonight; any normal girl who could restore my faith in the fairer sex.

The Treasury was relatively busy already. It was one of those places centrally located in the high street so it got a fairly good mix of people. I found my friends in the high seats by the bar and sat down and ordered a drink. I felt so much more invigorated and restored after the long walk. I took one sip of my pint and across the room I saw a familiar face. It was a girl who used to go out with one of my friends but broke up with him not so long ago. She was radiant and I knew that she was the girl I needed to talk to tonight. Her name was Jo.

Jo was a wonderful girl. She was a woman in her own right, yet still touched by innocence and sweetness; it was as if her aura was composed of nothing but pureness and goodness. A strong description I know, but Charlie was so used to seeing girls in this area destroyed by drunken men and plagued by premature desires of family and childbirth. Some were sedated by their parents, attempting to rectify their shortcomings, through the lives of their children. Jo seemed to transcend all of this. Of course, she had enjoyed the flights of fancy her city nightlife had afforded her. She would have some skeletons in her closet and have regrets like everyone else. But as Charlie looked at her in this moment, none of that seemed to matter.

She looked over at him and pondered how to spend the following few hours. She didn't know him properly, but she was intrigued by him. The decision she made, like any girl of that age, was the wrong one.

29

In Charlie's mind there was only one thing that he could possibly do to justify the balance of what had happened. He needed to know what had happened to his wife; he needed to find out who was responsible for her disappearance. It had been discussed by the authorities that she may just have left. However, Charlie knew his wife and thought it would not be likely. There was no reason for her to leave and also in such an abrupt fashion. All her clothes were still in the house where she had left them, so it seemed illogical. Charlie knew in his gut who had the answers to his questions and he was determined to find her. He picked up the phone and began dialling.

"Hello mate, how are you?" answered the voice on the other line.

"Ok. Look, I need you to find someone for me. It's a name that is familiar to you," said Charlie. His friend on the other line had access to confidential information not many people could get hold of, due to his line of work.

"Ok, who is it?" he asked.

"It's Bobby. Helen Roberts."

"Her? Why are you looking *her* up?" asked the voice on the other end of the line.

"Ask me no questions..." Charlie replied.

"Hmm...ok...give me half an hour."

Charlie put the phone down and waited in silence. He was so engulfed with anger that the rest of his thought processes had become unimportant. He was numb and mechanical about his movements since Jo had disappeared and he was pleased about this. He didn't want to stop hating or wanting revenge. If he did, he would probably break down.

He started loading his car with the things he would need for the journey. Charlie had no idea where Helen would be, although he had an inkling she would be somewhere in the Home Counties. She had family in Worcestershire and it was a possibility she had moved somewhere near there, Malvern for instance, but that seemed more unlikely. Charlie grew impatient waiting for the phone to ring. He went upstairs and locked all the windows individually and made sure the curtains were drawn. The last few weeks had made him meticulous about security. No matter what happened, he would never make the same mistakes again.

The phone rang.

"Yeah, I have got her."

"Where is she?" Charlie said with menace in his voice.

"She is currently living on the outskirts of Maidstone with her mother and father. I can give you the address."

Charlie jotted down the address.

"Oh, something else of interest for you Charlie,"

"What's that?" he replied.

"Well, she is studying at the moment."

"Oh, that is a bit of a surprise. Where is she?" Charlie retorted.

"It is term time, so you might want to check out Canterbury Christ Church University. It says she has signed up for a day course there for another year at least."

"I see. Thanks, I appreciate that." Charlie said genuinely.

"Charlie, you need to be careful...don't do anything that..."

"I won't. Thanks again." Charlie put the phone down.

Canterbury? Back where it all started, how fitting, Charlie thought. He put on his leather jacket, took one last look around his front room, glancing at the black and white wedding picture on the side and left for the motorway.

Charlie knew the way back to Canterbury like the back of his hand. He cruised down the A2 at 70mph, not wishing to attract undue attention. He thought about stopping in at Maidstone first, but as it was a Wednesday it seemed highly unlikely she would be there. It sounded like she was not in halls and she was commuting to university, but it seemed probable that she was in lectures now.

Charlie got out his phone and dialled. He should have known he would be talking to an automated voice service; however nothing was going to deter him from finding the answers he needed. Finally, he heard a woman's voice.

"Hello, Christ Church?"

"Oh, hi there. I am trying to locate my niece, I believe she is in one of the lectures today, I am meeting her for lunch. Can you tell me where she might be?" Charlie asked politely.

"Hold on, one second. What is the name please?"

"Helen Roberts, she may be known as Bobby. Bobby Roberts."

"Hold the line sir."

Charlie was more than happy to hold if he was to get the answer he wanted.

"Yes sir, she is in the Coleridge building at present. But she breaks for lunch in twenty five minutes so you can probably catch her then. Did you want me to leave a message for her?"

"No, no. Thanks for your help."

30

Charlie waited at the back entrance of the University for Helen to appear. He waited in the car because she wouldn't recognise it and he wanted to go unnoticed for as long as possible.

He waited and watched the crowds of young students pile out of the gate, oblivious to the cruel realities awaiting them in the real world. He felt so disjointed at the moment, like in a hellish limbo, where he felt everyone was against him. He wanted to go back to the days when he was walking out of those gates and his only worry in the world was where the money for his next beer was coming from.

He saw her in front of him. She was in a group of four people and they headed in towards the town centre. Charlie jumped out of his car and followed behind them. Two of the group splintered off to the left towards the East of the city, while Helen and one other guy headed towards the city wall and into the Cathedral area.

Charlie watched as they crossed the busy ring road and made their way through the small doorway and into the Cathedral grounds. He waited for them to pass out of sight before jogging across the road himself and through the gate. He walked straight across the rose garden and saw the pair in the distance. It looked like they were kissing before the man turned and walked through the main Cathedral gate and into the town centre. Helen was by herself. This was Charlie's chance now.

She turned on her heel and headed towards the Cathedral. What was she doing? She headed inside the main door as Charlie bided his time before entering the building. It was lunchtime and was fairly busy, though Charlie tiptoed as lightly as he could whilst inside, as the stone floor and walls magnified every sound that was made. Charlie's heart was pumping and he felt as though something mysterious was about to unfold.

He followed her through the main part of the church, past the brown wooden pews and the main alter at the focal point of the building. She continued to walk through the church and headed past the golden statue of Thomas Becket and down into the Cathedral's crypt.

Charlie waited and moved to his right to light a candle at the side of the room. He was nervous and needed strength. He said a prayer for his father and for the safe return of his wife. He crossed himself and looked down at the glowing light rising from the base of the stairs, where the crypt lay.

He waited a further few minutes before quietly descending the stairs and waited by the open door of the room in front of him. He heard voices, both familiar and whispers in the darkness. He couldn't make out quite what was being said, but he could recognise the voices, two females he knew pretty well.

He pushed the door slightly ajar, it creaked loudly. The talking stopped.

"Is that you?" Helen whispered into the darkness and footsteps came towards the door. Charlie not wishing to be discovered, turned around and went to ascend the stairs and hide, but as he turned, he noticed the frame of an old friend in front of him, blocking his path. It was Ben.

"Hello Charlie. Remember me?" he asked with a smile on his face.

Before Charlie had a chance to move, Ben hit him with an iron pole across the face and Charlie dropped to his feet and down into the crypt.

31

Charlie awoke on a dirty mattress in the centre of a sterile room with white walls and no windows. He felt his face which was severely bruised and as he lifted his head from the pillow his head pounded severely. As he rose to his feet, he noticed a chair in the room and behind him was a big steel door.

He heard the sound of footsteps outside and voices before a metal clank and the door creaked open. Ben stood in the doorway.

"Hello again Charlie."

Charlie sized him up and he noticed Ben had got significantly bigger since the last time he saw him. That would be what jail time does to you, Charlie thought. He fancied his chances against Ben, but before he could plan a form of attack, he felt a surge of pain through his stomach, which brought him onto one knee.

"Before you even think about it Charlie, that is a form of tranquilizer going through your body. It's a little like ketamine, but without the fun parts, y'know? In a few moments, you won't be able to move." Ben stated.

Charlie tried to raise himself up but it was futile. He dropped onto the floor and propped himself up against the wall as best he could.

"It is best you listen to me, don't try to fight it. That is what your wife did to no avail. I felt pretty bad that it killed her baby, I didn't want that to happen, an unfortunate side effect I guess."

Charlie wretched and tried to lunge at Ben.

"Oh, you didn't know? Yes, Charlie she was pregnant, but not anymore I am afraid mate. I am surprised she didn't tell you? She wanted a girl, she wanted to call her Madison or Maddie. She must have been so excited about telling you..."

"Where is she?" Charlie forced out. He was beginning to sweat profusely and could no longer control his limbs. He tried to raise his arm, but it fell like lead to the stony ground.

"She is gone. I would forget about her, just like I had to forget about my life and my future thanks to you."

"Wh...What..?"

"You ruined my life Charlie, you ruined my love! Six years of my life wasted, rotting away! My one true love gone from me forever! Well, now it is your turn, you prick, to sit and wait and think about all you have lost and all that could have been for you." Ben spat out.

"But...I...what did I do..? Ben you fucked me over...you...tried to betray me..!"

"Did I? Maybe I did, maybe not. All that I know is that you are going to have a nice, long amount of time to think about everything that has happened. Because you didn't wipe away all of your footprints Charlie, some remained. And you need to pay for the mess you left and the life you lived, just like everyone else had to."

Ben left the room and shut the metal door behind him. Charlie was apoplectic with rage but he couldn't even move his head from the mattress. He closed his eyes as Ben's prophetic words raced around his head.

The sound of pattering feet woke me from a light and troubling sleep. As I rubbed my eyes awake, a bright white light immersed my face and senses. My face felt greasy and hot as I fell back to the mattress. I wrenched the cover over my head, only to feel it being yanked and pulled away from me, out of my grasp. I surrendered and opened my eyes, to see the face of an angel and a bright white light, streaming from behind her head. I thought I must be in heaven; I must be...until my senses kicked in and reality flooded me. It was my daughter, Madison, standing at the bedroom window, in front of a world carpeted with snow.

I started thinking of the day ahead and the errands I had to complete. My head pounded from the night before but as Madison ran down the stairs and called up to me; my heart filled with joy. I felt like I was a child again, begging my Dad to take me sledging on the hills.

I got up and plodded downstairs, wrapping myself up in warm clothes for the day. I took my first step in the snow and heard the crunch under foot; a beautiful, velvet carpet destroyed by my size 11 boot. We skipped across to the park, Madison slipping on the ice, falling and laughing. I could hear her voice *so* happy and excited as she threw snowballs at passers-by and parked cars.

I turned and looked at the bare trees, iced with snow, moving with the whispering wind. As I pondered this beautiful scene, I felt a crack in the face and tasted moisture in my mouth, as Madison giggled to herself. I chase her, following her footprints in the snow. I run and run, until darkness surrounds me. I am fighting against the wind, treading through water until my legs give way with pain and I fall to the floor. I realise that I am not in the park; Madison is not in front of me. My head swirls, my eyes open and I am back in the sterile room as the steel door in front of my clanks open.

I wake up covered in sweat as I feel for the side of the mattress. My breathing is fast and light; like a bird trying to escape from the treachery of my body. Like a soul trying helplessly, to rid itself from guilt.

I sit up and realise where I am. Those soul aches that steal us from sleep return, duller and angrier than ever. The steel clank of the opening door drags me back to actuality. I wait for a figure to appear in the doorway and for the next chapter in this dark episode.

Coming soon, from the same author,

THE CARNIVAL THAT ATE THE WORLD

Billy looked out of the bedroom window and saw the commotion at the end of his garden. The funfair had arrived in town and was setting up in Wicker Park, at the back of his house. He could see the workers moving like ants in-between the machinery, carrying boxes and electrical wires. Billy was jealous. He wanted more than anything to be a part of the Carnival worker's crowd. He though about the freedom their lifestyle offered them and like a child would, he imagined a life of bright lights, fast rides and non-stop excitement.

Billy pulled the curtains roughly and plonked himself down on his bed with a sharp sigh. *One more night* he thought to himself, before the carnival began. He lay down on the bed, wishing it was time to go to sleep *now*, so Friday could come quicker. All then he would have to do, was get through one more day of school and one more dinnertime, before he could race to the park and...

"Billy! Dinner's ready!" came the call from downstairs. Billy listened intently to the faint hum of excitement building at the bottom of his garden. He smiled to himself, before racing downstairs.

The alarm woke Billy at 7.15am. Today, he jumped straight out of bed and into the shower without his mum needing to call for him to get up. Normally, she would need to do this a few times before words made any impression and woke him from slumber. Today was different. Billy was already towelling himself down when his Mother ascended the stairs with a grimace on her face, to commence battle.

"Billy? Are you in the bathroom?" she enquired.

"Yes, ma – wont be a second!" he replied.

"Ok…you're lunchbox is by the front door. See you after school, son."

The day moved at snail's pace. He found himself clockwatching for the most part, or daydreaming about the wonders the carnival had to offer him tonight. Billy spent most of the day in his own little world. He didn't have many friends but nodded at a few of the boys he had become acquainted with and occasionally chatted to. Mostly though, at school, he kept himself to himself. He had a few mates he rode his bicycle with where he lived, but on the whole, he was a solitary type of person.

He watched as the second hand moved sluggishly around Miss. Wilson's clock. Billy had already planned what rides he was going on and what order he would do them in. He doodled in his book; drawing a juggling clown in front of a roller coaster he had named 'Whirling Thunder'.

RING!!!! There it was - the bell! Billy didn't wait to find out what his homework was. He looked at Miss. Wilson as she tried to stop him fleeing for the door, but it was to no avail, Billy was gone. He weighed it up in his mind and thought an hour's detention was probably worth it. Anyway, that was *next* week. He had the weekend in front of him and he wasn't going to waste a minute of it.

The stopper at the back of his piggy bank was difficult to dislodge, but Billy managed it and poured the contents over his bed. He counted it and was disappointed at what he found. $7.53. This wasn't anywhere *near* enough for a weekend at the carnival! Billy screwed his face up and his breathing quickened. He thought of how he would broach the subject with his Mother and whether she would be able to even lend him any quick money.

Suddenly, he had an even better plan. He quietly tip-toed down the stairs and saw his Mother's green handbag hanging at the bottom. He moved towards it checking the whereabouts of his Mother in the house. He couldn't hear her or see her, so he presumed she must be in the garden or getting something from the car. He reached for the bag and slowly pulled out her little purse. The newsreader on the TV was talking about the economy or something…Billy tried to focus on what he was doing and opened the metal clips slowly. He saw a wodge of notes and took one out as quickly as he could. Just as he put the purse back, he heard the brisk click-clack of his Mother's shoes on the kitchen floor. He dropped the bag in a panic, as its contents spilled all over the hallway floor.

"*Billy!*" came the saddened cry from the kitchen.

He looked up at his mother before bolting for the front door, her forlorn face the image etched into his mind as he made his way around the corner, to the Wicker Park fair.

As he walked down the street he could hear the sounds of the funfair luring him in like a siren's call. He rounded the corner to see the park in front of him and the thick green gates of the fair lie in the distance. Over the top of the gates he could see the top of the helter skelter flashing different colours. Blue, pink, green, violet. Billy was buoyed by this sight and raced ahead to the thick wooden gates of the fair. As he drew closer he saw two clowns, taking entry money at the gate.

Billy fished through his pocket to find some money and he found the note he stole from his Mother earlier. He pulled out the crumpled $5 note and thrust it hastily toward the sad-faced clown.

In a slow voice the clown said, "Here's your change, be a good boy now son and take care!"

Billy snatched the change and walked towards the rides in front of him. Billy had been building up this moment in his mind for days now and he was not disappointed.

In front of him he saw the Ferris wheel, lit up in yellow and red lights. They looked like coloured stars against the darkness of the American night sky.

Billy was in his element. He whirled around in the waltzers and climbed skyward on the Ferris wheel. He felt as free as a bird while the wind blew around his skin and bones, on this fair Friday evening. He didn't have a care in the world and he felt exhilarated, relaxed and pacified in equal measure.

After he had been on his four favourite rides, he took a breather and walked the perimeter of the park. He stopped at the cotton candy seller, a big portly man, who beamed a broad grin at young Billy.

"Hello, young man. Are you enjoying yourself at the fair?"
"Yessir!" replied Billy eagerly.
"Would you like some cotton candy, my boy?"
"Yessir, a big one please!"
The cotton candy seller turned to pick up one of his wooden sticks. As he did Billy rustled through his pockets to find some money. As he rustled through sweet wrappers and useless bits of paper, he started to panic as he found no sign of any money whatsoever. He tipped out his pockets to see if he had any shrapnel. He rooted around and managed to scrape together 37 cents. *37 cents!* What was he going to do with that?

He looked pleadingly up at the man behind the counter, who looked stern and folded his arms.
"Sorry sir…I…" Billy started.
"I am sorry young man, if you don't have means to pay, you can't have any cotton candy or any more rides at the fair."
"Wh…but…I thought… I…" Billy was mortified.
"I am sorry," the man stood firm.
Billy turned in a daze, before anger took control of him and he threw his 37 cents as hard as he could against the cotton candy stall. The coins chinked against the glass and metal, as the cotton candy seller shook his head in disappointment and turned away.

ABOUT THE AUTHOR

Trevor Warman is a new writer, who currently lives and works in South London.

'Footprints' is his first work of fiction and he is currently working on his second novel. He writes in a realistic and defined manner, merging his own personal experiences with an empathetic and unique style.

He also writes poetry and has completed two anthologies, as well as penning song lyrics and travel/music articles and reviews. More information about his writing can be found at the web site, http://tjwarman.ucoz.com.

Trevor Warman is one of the only exciting modern storytellers for an exciting modern generation.

Lightning Source UK Ltd.
Milton Keynes UK
08 June 2010

155274UK00001B/128/P